the
best
friend

Books by Melody Carlson

Just Another Girl

Anything but Normal

Never Been Kissed

Double Take

The Jerk Magnet

The Best Friend

Allison O'Brian on Her Own, vol. 1

Allison O'Brian on Her Own, vol. 2

Devotions for Real Life

Life at Kingston High

the best friend

Melody Carlson

Revell

a division of Baker Publishing Group
Grand Rapids, Michigan

© 2012 by Melody Carlson

Published by Revell
a division of Baker Publishing Group
P.O. Box 6287, Grand Rapids, MI 49516-6287
www.revellbooks.com

Printed in the United States of America

Library of Congress Cataloging-in-Publication Data
Carlson, Melody.
    The best friend / Melody Carlson.
        p.   cm. — (Life at Kingston High ; bk. 2)
    Summary: When high school junior Lishia Vance goes from being sur-
rounded by her friends one day to a social outcast the next, without explanation, she discovers the treacherous world of friendship, loyalty, and choices.
    ISBN 978-0-8007-1963-0
    [1. Best friends—Fiction. 2. Friendship—Fiction. 3. High schools—Fiction.
4. Schools—Fiction. 5. Christian life—Fiction.] I. Title.
PZ7.C216637Bes 2012
[Fic]—dc23   2011050220

Scripture quotations are from the Contemporary English Version © 1991, 1992, 1995 by American Bible Society. Used by permission.

12   13   14   15   16   17   18   7   6   5   4   3   2   1

one

ishia Vance grimaced to see that her regular lunch table was nearly full. As usual, no one had saved a place for her. Well, except for that pathetic little spot down on the end of the bench. As she sat down, squeezing herself onto about four inches of bench, completely unnoticed by her so-called friends, she wondered what was wrong with her. Why had everyone turned against her this year?

She sighed as she shoved her straw into her soda. It had been bad enough to get dumped by her boyfriend last summer, but shortly after that her best friend had dropped her as well. What an impressive way to start her junior year at Kingston High! Now, several weeks later, Lishia's self-esteem had plummeted so low that she found herself schlepping from class to class. Even now she kept her eyes on her tray, not saying a word to her "friends." Not that they seemed to notice or care.

This social isolation was taking its toll on her, and she wondered what had become of the happy girl she used to be. She felt like someone had nuked her life when she wasn't looking. Like one day everything was totally cool, and the next day . . . it was over.

On a good day, which was rare, she could admit to herself that the breakup with Daniel had been for the best—especially after he dropped out of youth group last summer. However, truth be told, Lishia did not miss Daniel nearly as much as she missed her best friend. And she wasn't dumb. She had seen it coming. Last summer Janelle had started hanging with her neighbor (a drop-dead gorgeous girl who'd just moved in), and suddenly those two were inseparable. Naturally, Lishia was left out in the cold. Who wouldn't have felt hurt?

"I'm just trying to be a good Christian and a good friend to Chelsea." Janelle would use this as her excuse each time she declined Lishia's invitations to do something. Janelle always claimed it was because Chelsea was new in town and she was lonely. Like Lishia wasn't lonely?

Janelle had seemed oblivious to the fact that Lishia had been in real pain and was even struggling with her faith as a result. But, as usual, Lishia kept her feelings to herself, pulling further away as she watched Janelle and Chelsea's friendship growing stronger. It didn't help that Chelsea Martin was a knockout or that all the youth group kids seemed strangely drawn to her. And it had only grown worse when school started. Sometimes Lishia felt like she hated—seriously hated—Chelsea Martin.

Lishia knew it was wrong to feel like that. As a Christian, she should be above petty jealousy. Shouldn't she? Or maybe she was just fooling herself. Because the truth was, Lishia not only envied Chelsea, but she secretly imagined unfortunate things happening to the vivacious girl. Oh, not anything horrible like death or dismemberment, but it would be delightful to see Chelsea emerge from the restroom with, say, a trail of toilet paper dragging from the backside of her jeans. Or maybe Chelsea could break out in big ugly hives, or get an enormous zit on the tip of her perfect nose, or simply have a bad hair day. Not that any of this was likely. If anything, Lishia was the one who seemed more subject to those sorts of predicaments.

Even today, as she'd passed by Chelsea (who'd been sitting in the center spot at the lunch table, relaying some enthralling tale), Lishia had controlled herself from "accidentally" tilting her tray and allowing her large Sierra Mist to topple over and splat right down on that beautiful blonde mane of hair. Instead, Lishia had played the role of the mouse and was now quietly sitting here feeling alone and left out—and bitter. And it was all Chelsea's fault. Lishia glanced over at the laughing girl, wishing she'd gag on her cheeseburger and vomit all over everyone.

Lishia looked away and, biting her lip, reprimanded herself for harboring such evil thoughts toward Chelsea. Really, what was happening to her? It was like her faith was slipping right between her fingers. Like if she wasn't careful, she might lose it altogether. Maybe she already had.

Lishia studied her "friends" and wondered what they would think if they knew how precarious she felt right now. After all, they were supposed to be Christians . . . but did they care about her or how she was suffering? It sure didn't feel like it.

Okay, to be honest, not all of her youth group friends had totally ignored her. In fact, Megan Bernard had actually gone out of her way to be friendly a number of times. But Lishia had never really liked Megan that much. She was kind of a blabbermouth and had absolutely no sense of style. Still, Megan might be better than having no friends at all.

As Lishia unwrapped her burrito, she had to admit that she was probably as much to blame for her friendless state as anyone. But it was like she was trapped, feeling more and more out of sorts and more and more left out, like she had created this wall around herself and now had no idea how to get over it. If only someone else would try to knock it down for her. Wasn't that what friends were supposed to do?

She took a bite of her burrito and wished she was a stronger Christian—the kind of person who became stronger through her trials, able to forgive and forget and move on with her life. It shouldn't be this difficult, should it? It wasn't as if she wasn't trying to be a stronger Christian. Out of real desperation, she'd started to study her Bible, reading about "the fruit of the Spirit." She'd even memorized the character qualities. As she chewed, she ran the list through her head. *Love, joy, peace, longsuffering, kindness, goodness, faithfulness, gentleness, and self-control.* Those were great-sounding qualities, and she wanted them in her life. However, she wasn't quite sure how to get them.

And just now, feeling forced to overhear Janelle and Chelsea's retelling of their "big adventure"—some crazy stunt they'd pulled off at last weekend's youth group retreat (the same retreat that Lishia, feeling friendless, had boycotted)—felt like way too much longsuffering. Seriously, her patience was wearing thin. Why didn't her friends care about how left out she felt right now?

She considered that list of qualities as she took a slow sip of soda, but it only frustrated her more. Her chances of exhibiting love and kindness were steadily shrinking. She didn't feel a milliliter of joy or goodness about anyone or anything today. The only kind of fruit she was going to experience was the Granny Smith apple on the corner of her lunch tray.

She took one slow last look at her oblivious friends, then picked up her tray and bag and simply walked away. She didn't say a word to anyone. Not that anyone would care, since they were so entranced by the story Chelsea and Janelle were regaling them with, going on about how they'd dressed up like other people and pulled off some kind of crazy charade at the retreat. She could hear their laughter as she walked away—not directed at her, of course, but excluding her all the same. As she crossed the cafeteria, she realized the most irksome part about walking away was that no one bothered to question why she was leaving before finishing her lunch. The sad truth was that no one even seemed to notice.

With a lump in her throat and a rock in her stomach, Lishia decided to dump her half-eaten lunch. But on her way to the trash can, she noticed Riley Atkins sitting alone. Slightly hunched over with her eyes downward, Riley stared at her green salad as if it were the most interesting object on earth. Lishia stopped in her tracks to stare at this oddity—not that Riley was infatuated with her salad, but that Riley was by herself. Because Riley Atkins *never* sat by herself. At least not to Lishia's knowledge. Riley was usually smack-dab in the middle of a small crowd of boisterous and popular kids. It simply was what it was—and there were reasons why.

For starters, Riley was a popular cheerleader. That alone seemed to demand the company of a few friends. Lishia knew this from experience since she'd been a cheerleader once too, way back in middle school. Besides that, Riley had a high-profile boyfriend. At least she used to—Lishia wasn't so sure about that now. Dayton Moore, star football player at Kingston High, had been Riley's main squeeze for ages. And Dayton almost always attracted a small crowd. But now he was over there and Riley was alone. Something was definitely wrong.

Lishia was nearly to the trash cans when she turned around to study Riley again. Maybe it was her imagination, but something about Riley's demeanor looked so sad and downhearted that Lishia knew she needed to at least inquire. After all, Riley and Lishia had been pretty good friends back in middle school. And although they weren't really friends now, they still exchanged words sometimes.

"Hey, Riley," Lishia said gently.

Riley looked up with sad blue eyes. "Hey, Lishia." Her voice sounded dull and a little rough around the edges.

"Anyone sitting here?" Lishia gave her a hopeful smile.

Riley shrugged. "Doesn't look like it, does it?"

Lishia took this as an invitation and sat down across from her. "You okay?"

Riley let out a long, sad sigh. "Not exactly."

"I'm sorry." Lishia took a sip of her soda. "Want to talk about it?"

Riley looked a bit suspicious now.

"Or not." Lishia shrugged. "Although we *used* to be friends." She picked up her half eaten burrito and took a bite.

"Why aren't you sitting with your *youth group* friends?" Riley asked with a slightly accusing tone, as if there was something wrong with being part of youth group. And for all Lishia knew, maybe there was.

Lishia chewed slowly as she tried to think of an answer less humiliating than the truth.

"Please don't tell me you're on some kind of mission to save me." Riley's voice suddenly grew irritated. "Because I really can't handle that right now, if you don't mind."

"No way." Lishia shook her head and swallowed. "I just thought you looked lonely."

"Just because I'm sitting alone does not mean I'm lonely." Riley glared at her. "Maybe I'm tired of all the noise."

Lishia nodded. "Well, the truth is, I'm feeling kinda lonely today."

Riley seemed caught off guard. "Really? You're lonely?"

"Yeah." To her own surprise, Lishia opened up by confessing about how she'd been replaced as Janelle's best friend. "Chelsea Martin is nice and all, but I just feel so—"

"Are you kidding me?" Riley slammed down her fork with a vengeance. "I *hate* that stupid Chelsea Martin."

"Seriously?"

"She's the one who messed things up between Dayton and me."

"So you and Dayton aren't together anymore?"

She rolled her eyes. "Hadn't you heard?"

"And Chelsea is the reason?" Lishia leaned forward with interest. "How so?"

"When she first moved here, Dayton and I were about to get back together. You know, right before school started. But suddenly he was like totally smitten by this new girl. Of course, I figured it all out as soon as I saw him gaping at her." Riley scrunched up her nose. "I mean, sure, I suppose she's pretty hot . . . that is, if you like *that* kind of look, which Dayton obviously seems to appreciate." She shook her head.

Lishia tried not to laugh because the truth was, Riley's look wasn't all that much different from Chelsea's—in that blue-eyed blonde babe sort of way. But to be honest, though Lishia wasn't about to admit it, Chelsea was probably prettier than Riley.

"Then, even though Chelsea wasn't interested in Dayton, he kept obsessing over her, like he actually thought he was going to win her over just by drooling and acting like a total idiot. Well, after a while, I couldn't take it anymore. I told Dayton to forget it, that I'd never go back even if he was the last guy on the planet."

"All because of Chelsea?"

Riley nodded as she took a bite of her salad.

"So that's why you're sitting alone now?" Lishia felt confused. It sounded like she and Dayton had broken up a while back.

"No, that is not why I'm sitting alone now." Riley sounded aggravated, as if whatever was troubling her should be obvious.

"Oh . . ." Lishia decided to focus on finishing her lunch and moving on. It seemed that talking to Riley was a bad idea.

"I'm sorry," Riley blurted unexpectedly. "I didn't mean to hurt your feelings. It's just that my friends have been so cruel to me."

Lishia looked up. "Your friends are cruel to *you*?" Usually Riley's friends saved their meanness for girls like Lishia. Picking on Riley gave it a whole new twist—and in a twisted way, it was oddly refreshing. Not that Lishia planned to mention it.

Riley nodded with misty eyes. "In fact, Amanda just told me off." She sniffed indignantly. "Right in front of everyone too. I've never been so humiliated in my life."

Lishia blinked. "Amanda told you off?" Amanda Jorgenson, also a cheerleader, was usually the nicest one of that particular group—maybe even the nicest girl in the whole school. Lishia thought that Amanda and Riley were pretty close friends. Maybe even best friends. Lishia couldn't imagine Amanda telling off Riley like that. "Why would she do that to you?"

"All because of stupid Gillian." Riley glanced over her shoulder toward the noisy table where her friends were seated. "I hate her!"

Now Lishia felt confused. "Amanda was mean to you because of Gillian Rodowski?"

Riley scowled as she stabbed her fork into a cucumber slice like it was a Gillian Rodowski voodoo doll.

"But why?"

Riley slammed down her fork. "Because I simply made a perfectly innocent comment."

"A comment?"

"About Gillian's total lack of loyalty."

"Loyalty to what?"

"To *me*." Riley narrowed her eyes. "Haven't you heard that Gillian and Dayton started dating recently?"

"I guess I missed that one too."

"Well, they did. They got together last weekend. And Gillian knew full well that I wanted to get back with him. Just the same, she put the move on him, and now it's really over between Dayton and me."

Lishia wasn't sure how to respond. Hadn't Riley just said that it was over and she wouldn't take him back if he was the only guy on earth? Still, Lishia didn't want to appear unsympathetic. "I'm sorry," she said quietly. "That must've hurt."

Riley nodded, picking up her fork again.

"I guess we have something in common," Lishia told her. "We both feel like outsiders today."

Riley peered curiously at Lishia. "It must be even harder on you."

"Huh?" Lishia wasn't sure what Riley was referring to.

"I mean not being a cheerleader anymore. At least I still have that."

Lishia shrugged. It was bad enough feeling like she'd lost her boyfriend and best friend this fall; she didn't want to be reminded of an uncomfortable memory now. She'd been such a fool to try out for varsity cheerleading last spring. Really, what had she been thinking?

"You know, you used to be really good, Lish. I mean, back in middle school," Riley said. "Don't you ever miss it?"

"Sometimes I do," Lishia admitted. "But I know it's a lot of work too."

"Tell me about it."

"So I'm okay with cheering from the sidelines." Lishia forced a smile. The truth was, she sometimes felt envious of the cheerleaders, kicking and jumping in their purple-and-white uniforms. She wondered if perhaps she'd practiced a bit more, taken it a little more seriously . . . would she have made the team? Back then Janelle had made fun of her for even trying, making comments like "Cheerleaders can jump high because their heads are full of hot air."

Riley's brow creased like she was thinking hard. "You know, you were really good at tryouts last year, Lishia."

"Thanks." Lishia felt her smile grow more genuine. That was high praise coming from someone like Riley.

"I think you actually came pretty close to making the team."

Lishia sighed. "Maybe so, but like my dad says, close is only good in horseshoes and hand grenades."

Riley looked amused. "Hey, does your dad still have that horseshoes pit in the backyard?"

Lishia nodded.

"Remember that slumber party you had at the end of eighth grade?" Riley gave a mischievous grin.

"When the boys crashed?"

Riley nodded. "Your dad was so outraged."

"And I got grounded too."

"Yeah, I remember." Riley's eyes twinkled. "Did you ever figure out who invited them?"

Lishia pursed her lips, then pointed an accusing finger at Riley. "You?"

She started to giggle. "Yep."

Lishia chuckled. "Remember when you pushed Dillon into the pool with his clothes on—and he was wearing his brother's letterman jacket?"

Riley was laughing harder now. "He deserved it after what he did to me."

Before long, they were both laughing hard as they started reminiscing about some funnier times—back when they'd been better friends.

"I'm glad you decided to sit with me," Riley said after the laughter settled down. "I feel a lot better now."

"Me too." Lishia wadded up her burrito wrapper and finished the last dregs of her soda.

"We should do this more often."

Lishia looked curiously at Riley now. "Really?"

"Sure. Why not? We used to be pretty good friends," Riley assured her. "I don't see why we can't be friends again."

Lishia was thoroughly shocked but trying not to show it. "You're serious?"

"Totally." Riley stood now, reaching for her bag. "What're you doing after school today?"

Lishia shrugged. She didn't want to admit that she was doing absolutely nothing—or that since her mom had gone back to work, the school bus was her main means of transportation. "Not much."

"If you can wait for me until after cheerleading practice, we can catch up some more."

Lishia nodded nervously. She knew that Riley had a car and could probably give her a ride, but she didn't want to ask. That would seem pathetic. "Sure, that'd be cool." But even as she said this, she wondered if Riley's offer was genuine. What if she was just punking Lishia?

"So meet me at the girls' gym after school, okay?"

"Okay . . ." Lishia agreed tentatively.

"Cool!" Riley looped the strap of her bag over a shoulder and headed off toward the door. As usual, and like all her friends did, she left her messy lunch tray on the table—as if she thought someone in the cafeteria had been hired to personally pick up after her.

Still feeling somewhat stunned by all this, Lishia gathered up both of their trays, carrying them to the trash and recycling area. As she disposed of the lunch junk, she started constructing a plan. After school, she'd "waste" some time in the library, maybe do homework for an hour or so. Then she'd wander into the gym and act nonchalant, just in case Riley had forgotten her promise to give her a ride—and in case Riley's offer was insincere or, worse yet, a heartless trick. Lishia might be friendless, but she still had some pride.

For that reason Lishia put together a worst-case-scenario plan—to be implemented if Riley pulled a mean girl act. Lishia would kill some additional time, maybe hanging in the art department while she waited for her mom to come by to pick her up. Although her mom only taught half days, she usually stayed at the school into the afternoon to work on lesson plans, or else she ran errands. Her theory was that being on her own would help Lishia become more independent. Lishia knew she could hoof it home if she had to, except, of course, that the forecast called for rain. But if Lishia wound up getting sopping wet, it would simply teach her a good, hard lesson—*never trust girls like Riley Atkins!*

two

Lishia felt a conflicting mix of deep insecurities and high expectations as she walked to the girls' gym. She knew that was where the cheerleaders practiced every day after school and spectators were welcome. However, she wanted to put on cool and aloof airs, like she was simply passing through. Without even glancing at the team, she walked over to the bleachers and sat down, casually crossed her legs, and promptly opened her cell phone—a girl's best friend when feeling unsure or conspicuous. As usual, she had no new texts, just further evidence of being ditched by Janelle. So much for Christian love.

Despite having nothing new to read, she focused intently on her phone, acting as if she were reading the most entertaining texts and feeling like a complete phony. She listened to the sounds of cheer practice as they worked on a routine, pausing several times to restart it. She could hear some bickering going on between Gillian and Riley, and finally she glanced up to see Coach Glassman, dressed in pink warm-ups, standing with her hands on her hips as she shook her head with a disappointed expression.

"You girls know better than to bring your private squabbles to practice with you," she warned them. "We are a team, girls! I expect you to act like one."

"I'm sorry," Riley said in a sharp and defensive tone. "But Gillian started it by saying I was off beat when she was clearly the one who messed up the last time."

"I don't care who started it," Coach Glassman told her. "It's time to end it now. Let's go through it again—this time with no problems."

Riley looked slightly hurt as she stepped back into line. Lishia couldn't help but note the glimmer of victory in Gillian's eyes. Lishia decided to watch the team more carefully now. Curious as to who was really in the wrong here, she studied them as they restarted the routine.

To be fair, both girls seemed to be equal in their skills as they went through their cheer. And there was no denying that they were both very good. In fact, Lishia felt that next to Amanda, who had reigned supreme as head cheerleader for years, Riley and Gillian were probably next in line for that honor. It was too bad the two girls didn't get along better.

Or not. Suddenly Lishia remembered why she was here today. She was waiting for Riley. And it seemed obvious that Riley needed a good friend right now. She needed someone to be in her court, someone to show her some much-needed sympathy and appreciation . . . and loyalty.

Lishia decided that was exactly what she would do. She smiled as she remembered the fruits of the Spirit, reciting them to herself in her mind. Perhaps this was her perfect opportunity to put them to work. She would need those qualities if she wanted to be a good friend to Riley. That is, unless Riley was just punking her. She still wasn't completely clear about that. So far Riley hadn't even acknowledged her presence, but that was probably because she was focusing on their routines. Lishia could see that it really was hard work. And although a part of her tried to feel lucky that she wasn't out there with them (perhaps a case of sour grapes), another part of her was envious. She used to be a good cheerleader—and she'd enjoyed it. Too bad she'd allowed it to slip away.

When practice ended, Riley spotted Lishia and actually waved to her as she picked up her duffle bag and strolled over.

"You guys look good," Lishia told her.

"But did you see what happened?" Riley asked in a hushed tone. "I mean, how Glassman blamed me for Gillian's total lack of coordination?"

Lishia nodded. "It seemed kinda mean to pick on you."

"I just know Gillian is working her," Riley explained as she slipped a team hoodie over her tank top. "It's like Gillian is trying to turn Coach, as well as everyone else, against me."

"That's not fair." Lishia patted Riley on the back. "And you're so good. I watched you, Riley, and it looked like you were doing everything just right."

Riley smiled as she zipped her bag. "Thanks."

"Are you going to shower and change?"

"No way." Riley frowned toward the other girls, who were leaving the gym. "I can't stand being around Gillian one more minute than necessary. Seriously, I might say something to get me into trouble if I have to look at her smug, ugly face. I'd rather shower at home."

"That's understandable."

"Do you need a ride?" Riley asked as they headed for the west exit.

Relief washed over Lishia. "Sure. Thanks."

Riley continued to vehemently complain about Gillian as they walked toward the parking lot. Naturally, Lishia wholeheartedly agreed with her on all accounts. What else could she do? However, she felt a tinge of guilt since she really didn't know Gillian that well, and some of the things Riley was saying seemed a little harsh. But Lishia rationalized that she was simply showing her support for Riley. It seemed clear that Riley needed someone on her side right now—especially since it sounded as if the whole team was turning against her.

"You know what really gets me?" Riley said as she drove out of the parking lot. "Gillian isn't even keeping the cheerleaders' code of conduct."

"You're kidding." Lishia was shocked because everyone knew that Coach Glassman was very strict about the conduct code. "Why is she still on the team then?"

"I honestly think she has some kind of insider connection to Coach."

"Really?"

"Yeah. I remember hearing last year that her mom's a friend or relative or something."

"Well, that's just not fair." Lishia felt indignant for Riley's sake.

"Tell me about it!" As Riley slowed for a traffic light, she let loose with some bad language directed toward Gillian. Lishia knew that swearing was against the conduct code too, but she didn't want to mention it. Not that she approved, but in light of how unfairly Riley was being treated, it seemed understandable. Besides, Riley was saying these things in private.

"So what did Gillian do to break the code?" Lishia decided to gather some facts.

"For starters, she's totally a party girl, if you know what I mean."

Lishia nodded like she got this, but she thought that all the cheerleaders liked to party. She'd heard plenty of rumors, and that was just one reason she'd told herself she was better off not being on the team in high school.

"And you know how she lost all that weight last summer, don't you?"

"Weight?" Lishia didn't actually recall Gillian ever having a weight problem.

"Yeah, she'd put on about twenty pounds last spring, and I heard she used some kind of illegal diet drug, something like meth, to take it off. For all I know, she might still be using. That might explain her personality change. You know, why she's gotten so mean."

"Oh?"

"Uh-huh. And there's more. But it's like Glassman is totally blind when it comes to Gillian."

"Do you really think it's because of Gillian's mom?"

"It's the only thing that makes sense."

"But that's not fair."

"I know." Riley growled as she hit her fist against the steering wheel. "I wish there was something I could do about it."

"I suppose you can't exactly go to Coach Glassman," Lishia began thoughtfully. "But maybe you could take it to someone higher than her."

Riley nodded with an interested expression. "I could do that, couldn't I?"

"In fact, it seems like it would be your responsibility to let someone know what's up. I mean, for the good of the whole team. It's not right that everyone is pulled down to a lower standard just because Gillian's mom has some inside connection to the coach. And if she's doing drugs . . ." Lishia shook her head. "Well, that's not just wrong, it's dangerous."

"You're right. If Gillian messed up a throw or a pyramid, someone could fall and get hurt."

That wasn't exactly what Lishia meant by dangerous, since she was thinking more about Gillian's own health, but it was a good point all the same. Riley turned onto Lishia's street, and Lishia tried not to show her pleasure that Riley even remembered where she lived. It had been several years.

"I'd love to blow the whistle on Gillian, but I don't want to come across as tattling. Especially with the whole thing with Dayton, you know? Someone might think I was trying to get back at her and not take me seriously."

"That is awkward." Lishia nodded. "Maybe you could do it anonymously."

"Maybe . . ." Riley turned to Lishia as she stopped at a stop sign. Her eyes lit up as if she had an idea. "Or maybe . . . what if you did it? You could tell on her and no one would suspect your motives."

"Me?" Suddenly Lishia was worried. She had no intention of getting involved in something like this. Being a friend was one thing. Turning into an informer was something else.

"Sure. You could make an appointment with Mrs. Valmer and tell her everything."

Lishia took in a quick breath. "But what would I say? How would I explain why I was doing this?"

"I can tell you exactly what to say—and how to say it. I have all the information we need."

"But wouldn't they wonder how I knew about all this? I mean, I'm not even friends with Gillian. How would I have any credibility?"

"You'd just tell her that you're my best friend and that you've observed some things that are disturbing and that you felt someone needed to say something. You know, in a really innocent sort of way." She grinned. "If anyone has an honest face, Lishia, it's you. Plus, everyone knows you're one of the goody-two-shoes girls. No offense. I meant that as a compliment." She chuckled as if she wasn't really sure.

Lishia felt slightly flattered and slightly insulted. She liked the idea of being Riley's best friend, but the rest of it was a little disturbing. "I don't know, Riley. I mean, telling the vice principal a secondhand report about Gillian seems a little, well, dishonest."

"It figures you'd act like that." Riley scowled. "I thought I could trust you."

"You can trust me. It's just that I don't want to—"

"Oh, forget the whole thing." Riley turned abruptly into Lishia's driveway, bouncing the tires over the side of the curb. "I don't know what made me think you'd care enough about me to help me do—"

"No, that's not it," Lishia interrupted. "I *do* care about you. And I'd like to help you. It's just that I'm trying to wrap my head around this whole idea. I mean, I did see Gillian treating you badly today. That seemed really wrong. But I haven't actually *seen* anything else. At least not enough to make a complaint to the vice principal."

"Never mind." Riley gave Lishia an exasperated look. "Sorry I even asked."

"Don't be so quick to give up on me," Lishia reassured her. "I need to think about this. I need to find out more about Gillian and what she's doing."

"I can help you gather some evidence," Riley said eagerly. "It shouldn't be hard to do." She gave Lishia a mischievous smile. "And there's something else you should probably know."

"What?"

"I really shouldn't tell you."

"Come on," Lishia urged, suddenly curious.

"I'd have to swear you to total secrecy."

"You can trust me."

"Okay. No one is supposed to know this, and I would get in serious trouble if Glassman knew that I peeked into her computer." She pressed her lips together tightly as if reconsidering this disclosure.

"What?" Lishia urged.

"Do you swear you won't tell a soul?"

Lishia nodded.

"Well, guess who the first alternate cheerleader is this year?"

Lishia shrugged. "I have no idea."

Riley smiled slyly. "You."

"Oh." Lishia was completely surprised but didn't want to show it. "Really?"

"But everyone thinks it's Michelle Parkington."

"That would've been my guess."

"Well, that would be a disaster."

Lishia frowned. "Why's that?"

"Because Michelle is a total mess. I'm pretty sure she wouldn't even have a chance anymore. Everyone knows she's fallen in with the wrong crowd. I'll bet she can't even pass a drug test these days. Not to mention alcohol. She's even come to school drunk before, and she was suspended once. So, really, she's out."

Lishia actually felt sorry for Michelle. She knew her parents had divorced last year, and she'd probably been even more disappointed than Lishia had been not to make cheerleader, especially after trying so hard.

"Hey, that gives me an idea!" Riley's eyes lit up.

"What?" Lishia was starting to feel overwhelmed with all of Riley's ideas.

"How about if I start teaching you the routines?"

"Huh?" Lishia felt confused. "Why?"

"So you'll be all ready to take Gillian's place after she gets placed on suspension. You can step in and act like you're learning them, but everyone will be amazed at how quickly you catch on." Riley laughed.

"You don't really think that I'd take Gillian's—"

"It could happen, Lishia. And if it does, don't you want to be ready?"

"I, uh, I don't know. This seems kinda crazy to—"

"Think about it, Lishia. We'd be cheerleaders together again. Wouldn't that be totally awesome?"

"But it's such a—"

"Come on." Riley narrowed her eyes. "Don't be such a wet blanket. Do you fully understand what I'm saying right now? What I'm offering you?"

Lishia felt slightly dizzy as she gripped the door handle. How did their casual conversation in the cafeteria ever evolve to this? What was Riley asking her to do? And how could Lishia even consider such a thing?

"Don't you get it? Seriously, think about it. If Gillian is off the team, you'll finally get your chance." She let out a happy sigh. "In fact, I'm starting to think it was no coincidence that we sat together at lunch today. It's like it was meant to be. Like you're going to be cheerleader and this is how it's supposed to unfold."

Lishia gave a nervous giggle.

"You don't think so?"

She shrugged. "It's a lot to take in."

"Yeah, I know," Riley said reassuringly, like she understood. "But think about it, okay?"

"I will."

"And remember, you swore not to tell anyone."

"Of course, I won't."

"There's only one more football game, and it would be stupid to lose Gillian before the season ends, since it would mess up all our routines. But we could use that time as well as the break before basketball to teach you all the routines. Then you'd be ready to step in at our first game."

"This is so weird." Lishia felt slightly giddy now. Was it really possible that she'd be on the team for basketball season?

"But you are interested, right? I mean, you'd be crazy to let an opportunity like this slip past, don't you think?"

"Of course I'm interested. It's just hard to absorb all this."

"Well, then think about it. I'll call you later. Do you still have the same phone number? It's probably still in my phone since I never clean out my address book."

"Yeah, it's the same." Lishia opened the door.

"Great." Riley nodded as if satisfied with how this was going. "I'll call you after I've had a shower, and we can kick it around some more. We need to come up with a good plan."

"Okay . . ." Lishia wiggled her fingers in a wave and closed the door. Then, still feeling stunned, she stood there watching as Riley's little red Honda zipped off down the street. This seemed like a dream. A very weird dream. But at the same time, Lishia felt excited and pleased with this new development. And she hoped it was real. Going from feeling friendless and depressed to having Riley as her new best friend and getting to join the cheerleading team seemed comparable to winning the lottery.

As she retrieved the mail from the mailbox, she wondered about all that Riley had dangled before her. On one hand, it seemed too good to be true, and she was smart enough to know what that could mean. On the other hand, Lishia thought that perhaps she deserved this opportunity. Life had been kicking her around for the past several weeks. Maybe it was finally her time to shine in the sun! But at what price? Turning informant on Gillian? No matter what Gillian was into, Lishia wasn't sure she was comfortable with that. Something about it felt wrong. However, it was also wrong for Gillian to be on the team and breaking the conduct code . . . and getting away with it.

Lishia felt torn and confused as she went into the house. That made her wonder about God's take on this. How did this new development fit into his plans for her? Or did God even have plans for her? Earlier today, she'd been ready to abandon her faith altogether. Now that life held some promise, she wanted to believe that God was somehow involved in it. Perhaps he was completely behind the whole thing.

Maybe he had heard her desperate prayers in regard to her loneliness and wanted to give her a break after all. Had he seen the way her old friends were treating her and how she didn't fit in anywhere? Perhaps it was like she'd heard her youth pastor say recently—God wanted her to step out of her old comfort zone and do something completely new. Why not?

Okay, she wasn't absolutely sure about all this, but she liked the sound of it, because for some reason she felt the need to put God's seal of approval on this new friendship with Riley. She wanted to believe this was a good thing. Not that she had any specific misgivings. Not exactly. Although she did feel a tiny bit uncomfortable . . . Was she really ready to turn her back on Janelle and the rest of her friends? Would she be willing to simply walk away from them, kind of like she'd done in the cafeteria today? Did she really want to embrace something completely new like this? And if she did, what was the harm in that?

Mostly Lishia just wanted to believe that she was finally coming to a fork in what had been a pretty rough road recently. She wanted to reach the place where life got good again. And why shouldn't she?

It also seemed obvious that Riley needed her—she needed a dependable friend. And if Lishia was good at anything, it was at being a genuine friend. In fact, she remembered that when the youth pastor had been talking about various gifts last summer, he had pointed out that Lishia was someone with the gift of being a true friend. That had meant a lot to her then, but during the past couple of months, she'd begun to question it. Perhaps this was her big chance to put that gift to good use!

As she went to her room, she imagined herself becoming Riley's most true-blue friend, standing by her through thick and thin. Who knew? Lishia's friendship might even encourage Riley to come back to youth group again. She hadn't been involved since middle school. But miracles could still happen—wasn't this bizarre afternoon proof of that?

three

For no rational reason, maybe just out of an old habit, Lishia picked up her phone and started to call Janelle. She wanted to tell someone about today's strange new development. Then she remembered two things. One, Janelle was no longer her best friend, and two, Riley had sworn her to secrecy. Consequently she set her phone aside, opened the freezer, pulled out a carton of Goo-Goo Cluster, and stuck a spoon into it. At moments like this a girl needed ice cream!

As she pigged out, she ran the last conversation around in her head and finally decided that there was no harm in exploring this a bit further. Riley was in need of a friend. Lishia was available. She would simply take it one step at a time and see how it went. No big deal. What could it hurt?

Still, Lishia didn't mention any of this to Mom or Dad at dinner. As usual, they made small talk about their day. Dad complained about a guy who was slacking off at work. Mom complained about the price of gas and groceries. A couple of times Lishia almost let her news slip out, but then she stopped herself. She was still at odds with this idea, trying to wrap her head around the whole thing and what sort of role Riley expected her to play in it. Although it was possible that Riley had changed her mind by now. Maybe she'd realized it was a crazy plan.

As Lishia cleaned up the kitchen after dinner, she kept her cell phone in her pocket. Riley still hadn't called, and Lishia was feeling anxious. Riley probably was having second thoughts. Lishia's doubts might've put Riley off and now she was probably looking for someone else to become her friend and confidant. What if Lishia had blown it completely?

Lishia considered calling Riley but was afraid she might sound desperate. Okay, she was desperate. Still, she didn't want Riley to know that. She wanted to play cool and laid-back and willing to do whatever it took to secure this friendship . . . and perhaps a chance at cheerleading too. Because suddenly it seemed critically important—she wanted this and she wanted it badly. So much so that she might do anything to get it. Well, not anything. She wouldn't lie, cheat, or steal . . . or do anything illegal.

But maybe she'd turn snitch. For the sake of justice—at least that's what she told herself. Did that mean she was compromising? Lishia wasn't so sure. Mostly she didn't want to think about that now. And she didn't want to pray about it either. Was she trying to push God out of the picture? She didn't even know.

It wasn't until she was finishing up her homework that her cell phone finally rang. Trying not to sound overly eager after her caller ID informed her it was Riley, she calmly said, "Hey?"

"So whaddya think?" Riley jumped right in.

"You mean about your idea?" Lishia closed her laptop and

sat down on the edge of her bed. She felt a rush of anticipation, like she was on the brink of something big and life changing.

"Yeah. Are you in or out?"

Lishia giggled nervously. "In."

"Cool." Riley began explaining her plan. "You'll go to the game with me tomorrow night and you'll sit down in front, close to the field, so I can talk with you and stuff. I want people to see us together so that everyone will get that we're good friends again."

"Okay." Lishia had no problem with that. In fact, she couldn't wait to see some of her friends' reactions when they saw her hanging with the cheerleaders. If nothing else, it would give them something to talk about. Not that she cared so much—after all, they had quit caring about her.

"After the game, we'll go to Allegro's like everyone else. And I'm going to be on my best behavior with Gillian."

"Uh-huh."

"But if you get a chance to irritate her—you know, get under her skin—I hope you'll take it. I want her to start showing her true colors around more than just the cheerleaders."

"How am I supposed to do that?" This might be a challenge since Lishia wasn't usually confrontational with anyone.

"She hates to be criticized. Just say something critical."

"Like what?" Lishia couldn't imagine what she'd say. "I mean, I'm not really like that, and I don't want to sound phony."

"Don't worry, I'll coach you. There's a fine art to being snarky."

"Really?"

"Trust me, I'll give you some good ammo. Maybe we can write some notes on your hand."

"On my hand?"

"You know, on your palm, like for an exam."

"Oh . . . Do you actually do that?"

Riley laughed. "Me and everyone else in the school."

Lishia had never cheated on a test in her life. Not that she wanted to admit this to Riley.

"But never mind that. The point is, we need to start gathering evidence on Gillian. Give me your email address and I'll forward you the conduct code so you can look it over and see if you have any additional ideas for how to nail Gillian. I thought that we might be able to get something this weekend. You know Todd Reimer is having a birthday party, and I'm sure Gillian will be there since Dayton and Todd are good buddies. So I'll expect you to go with me, okay?"

"But I haven't been invited."

Riley rolled her eyes. "I'm inviting you."

"It's not your party."

"Fine. I'll make sure you get your own personal engraved invitation."

Now Lishia rolled her eyes.

"Just trust me, okay?"

"Okay . . . I guess. But you know I don't drink, Riley."

Riley laughed. "And as far as anyone else knows, neither do I. But I'm actually glad you don't drink. You will be the designated photographer."

"Huh?"

"To catch Gillian at a bad moment."

"Oh, yeah, right."

"Your phone has a camera, right?"

"Of course."

"Good. Make sure it's fully charged on Saturday."

"Okay." Once again Lishia's head was spinning. It seemed like Riley's brain functioned at high speed all the time.

"I'll pick you up for school tomorrow," Riley informed her. "And could you try a little harder to look like best friend material? I mean *my* best friend?"

"I—uh—I guess so."

"No offense, but you really need to raise the bar."

Lishia stood now, looking at her image in her dresser mirror. She did look a little dowdy. Even her long, auburn hair, usually one of her best features, looked frizzy and in need of a good conditioning. "I kinda let myself go recently," she admitted. "I was a little down, you know?"

"I understand, believe me. But it's time to step up your game now, okay? I need you to put your best foot forward. Can you do that?"

"Of course." Lishia stood a little straighter, staring into her hazel eyes as she started putting together a strategy to improve her appearance tomorrow.

"Good, because I'm counting on you. And don't forget, this is as much for you as it is for me, Lishia. This is a huge opportunity."

"Uh . . . yeah."

"Besides that, it's the right thing to do. It's not fair that someone like Gillian is allowed to break the rules just because her mom is best friends with Coach Glassman."

"That's true." Lishia was about to ask Riley if she knew that for sure or if there was a way to prove it, but Riley had to go.

"See you in the morning!"

Lishia hung up the phone, then went into the bathroom where the light was brighter and she was able to do a more thorough inventory of her appearance. Really, it shouldn't be too hard to remedy this. She was blessed with a fairly good complexion. Although she didn't much care for her slightly snubbed nose or what her friends often called her "pixie face," she realized there wasn't much she could do about that. Instead she took a shower, giving her hair a thorough conditioning, and then gave herself a facial with an old product that her mom had tried and didn't like.

With her face still coated in green goo, she now began to dig through her closet, trying to come up with a good outfit for tomorrow. It wasn't that she didn't have the right clothes exactly (at least she hoped not), but it had been so long since she'd hung up or even washed her clothes that the pathetic heap, piled about two feet high inside her closet, looked overwhelming. Mom had taught Lishia to do her own laundry last year when she'd abandoned home to rejoin the workforce. But Lishia missed the good old days and still dragged her heels about approaching the laundry room. She knew if she played it just right, Mom would take pity and do the laundry for her like she did last time.

"What's up with you?" Mom asked curiously when she saw Lishia hauling out an overloaded laundry basket and with the pea-green facial cream still on her face.

"Just cleaning up my act," Lishia told her.

Mom smiled and patted her on the head. "Good for you!"

Lishia rolled her eyes.

"We're watching an old movie if you want to join us," Mom said as she poured some microwave popcorn into a bowl.

"I can't join you, I have to do my laundry," Lishia growled. "All by myself."

Mom laughed. "I'd offer to help, but I'm sure you can

handle it just fine. But if you have any questions, you know where to find me."

Lishia slogged on to the laundry room and dumped the contents of her basket onto the floor, trying to remember how this was done. She knew she was supposed to sort lights from darks and "when in doubt, wash everything in cold water." But the dials and buttons on the washing machine looked slightly overwhelming. "Mom!" she called out, hoping they hadn't started their movie yet. Soon Mom appeared and gave her a refresher course on how to do laundry as she helped her sort.

"And if you don't want something to shrink, don't put it in the dryer, or just put it in for a little while."

"Okay, okay." Lishia poured in the soap and pushed the on button. "I think I got it."

However, it was close to midnight when she finally finished the daunting task of doing her own laundry, and when she pulled her favorite jeans out of the dryer, the ones she'd planned to wear tomorrow, she could tell right away that they had shrunk. So had several of her favorite shirts! She went to bed ticked.

In the morning she scrambled to put together an outfit that would appease Riley. It wasn't easy and took about a dozen changes, but by the time she emerged from her room, she thought it was a success. She'd put a Gap skirt over leggings with boots, then topped it with a Banana Republic sweater. Not Lishia's usual look, but it reminded her of outfits she'd seen Riley and her friends wear. Besides that, her conditioning treatment of her hair had produced shiny results, and with a little mascara, blush, and lip gloss, she felt like she was at the top of her game again. It felt good!

Even Mom noticed. "Wow, you look nice this morning,"

she told Lishia as she handed her a small glass of orange juice. "But aren't you running late? The bus should've been here by—"

"Riley Atkins is giving me a ride."

Mom's brows arched. "Riley Atkins?"

Lishia nodded as she chugged down the juice.

"You and Riley are friends again?"

"Yeah." Lishia frowned. "Is that a problem?"

"No, of course not." Mom smiled. "In fact, I think it's nice." She pointed to a plate on the breakfast bar. "There's some toast if you want. Dad didn't have time to finish it."

"No thanks." Lishia glanced out the window to see Riley's car pulling up. "There she is."

"Then take a piece with you," Mom urged.

"Later," Lishia called as she dashed out. Did Mom think she wanted to arrive at school with toast crumbs all over her sweater or dark brown whole grains stuck between her teeth?

"Hey." Riley grinned. "You clean up good."

"Thanks." Lishia slid into the seat and smiled. "I guess I'd been so bummed that I kinda let myself go the past several weeks."

"Well, my theory is that you can only feel as good as you look. If you make an effort to look great, you should feel great. Don't you think?"

"I hope so."

"Okay." Riley switched gears. "I started to make a list of Gillian's weaknesses. You know, so we can start working on some good one-liners to get her with." She pointed to a piece of paper on the dashboard.

Lishia took it and began reading aloud. "One, occasional acne that she tries to cover with too much makeup in a shade that's too dark for her complexion. Two, weight issues and her illegal use of drugs to keep the pounds off. Three, family problems (parents recently split up and her dad has a slutty girlfriend). Four, big butt." Lishia started to laugh, then stopped herself. "That's a bit harsh, Riley."

"Hey, someone called her bubble butt once and she threw a total hissy fit. If Coach had seen her, she would've been suspended for sure."

Lishia continued going over the list. "A lot of these items seem focused on her weight, Riley. Doesn't that seem kinda mean? Seriously, am I supposed to point out that her *calves* are too big?"

"We have to hit her where it hurts in order to see her true colors."

"But let's be realistic. I can't really mention these things. Besides being mean, it feels phony."

"What about number seven?" Riley asked.

"BO?" Lishia frowned.

"Body odor. Believe me, after a workout that girl smells nasty. So you could say something innocent like, 'What is that smell?'" Riley chuckled. "And then you could realize it's Gillian and act all embarrassed, and if it makes you feel better, you could even apologize to her—after she blows up. You know?"

Lishia giggled. "I suppose I could do that . . . maybe."

"But don't do anything to start with. First you'll have to win her trust to get her guard down." Riley sounded like she'd had a lot of experience with these tactics.

"How do I win her trust?"

"With compliments. Gillian is so insecure that she just eats up praise. So if you get the chance, go ahead and lather it on tonight. Keep in mind that the list is mostly for later. Why don't you stick it in your bag for now . . . like ammo."

Lishia tucked the paper into a zippered pocket for safe-keeping. Hopefully she wouldn't actually need it. If Gillian was as mean as Riley was saying, she'd probably show her real self without too much provocation. And like Riley said, first of all Lishia needed to gain her trust.

However, Lishia didn't really know Gillian that well. Oh, she'd been in class with her and had probably exchanged words with her before, but Gillian had gone to a different middle school, and other than Lishia's first impression (that Gillian was a bit of a snob), she had little to go on. Well, other than what Riley had told her. Hopefully that information was accurate. As far as winning this girl's trust, that shouldn't be too difficult. Lishia had catered to Janelle's ego over the past couple of years, and Janelle could be a pain at times. Anyway, Lishia knew how to make a person feel special. But usually she was sincere when doing so. Perhaps there was a way to be sincere with Gillian as well. Because as much as she wanted a friend in Riley, she wasn't convinced that she wanted it badly enough to hurt someone else.

four

I love what you're doing with your hair," Lishia told Gillian at halftime. The cheerleaders were back in the stands now, taking a break, drinking from water bottles and retouching their lip gloss. It was the third compliment Lishia had paid Gillian, and judging by the girl's creased brow, she was growing suspicious. Maybe it was time for Lishia to back off. But who didn't like hearing a little praise about themselves?

"What is it with you?" Gillian said to Lishia as she tossed her water bottle back into her duffle bag. "It's like you're suddenly stalking me. Or maybe you have a crush on me." Gillian laughed. "Better not let Dayton hear about it."

"Sorry." Lishia forced an uneasy smile. "I just thought the highlights in your hair looked really good and I was curious, who does it for you?" She nervously patted her own long hair. It was still in its natural state, a nice auburn shade that she usually got compliments on. As a result, she'd avoided chemicals. "I—uh—I've been thinking I should get some highlights too."

Gillian frowned at Lishia's hair. "Yeah, it wouldn't hurt to perk up those mousy tones." Then she reluctantly told her the name of a salon.

"Is it really expensive?" Lishia was feeling sincerely curious. Maybe she was wrong about her hair. Perhaps she should look into this for real. No one had called her hair mousy before. But it was time for the cheerleaders to get back out to the field for a dance routine. Lishia smiled and waved and, feeling a little foolish, stood there on the sidelines with several other girls. Like them, she probably looked like a cheerleader groupie. The price one paid for friendship.

By the end of the football game, which they were losing, it seemed like Gillian was finally warming up to her a little. "Are you coming to Allegro's?" she asked Lishia as she gathered up her things and pulled on her letterman jacket.

"Yeah, I guess so." Lishia glanced over to Riley now. So far the two had barely spoken, and Lishia wasn't even sure how she was supposed to handle this. Was Gillian supposed to think that she and Riley weren't friends?

"Well, guess I'll see you there." Gillian actually smiled now. And it seemed almost genuine.

"Okay." Lishia even waved as Gillian and several of the others left together.

"Nice work," Riley said as she joined Lishia.

"I can tell they're really distancing themselves from you," Lishia admitted as they left the stadium. "Like they're trying to freeze you out."

"Tell me about it." Riley let out a long, sad sigh. "It's kinda like having your own family disown you. And it's all because of Gillian."

Lishia wanted to point out that Gillian was actually starting to seem somewhat nice—at least once Lishia had pressed through the ice princess act. But she knew that was not what Riley wanted to hear. Instead Lishia sided with Riley, agreeing that the treatment she was getting from her fellow cheerleaders was totally unkind and unfair.

"Especially considering that you guys are supposed to be a team," Lishia said as she got in Riley's car. "How can you be a team if there's this nasty quiet squabble going on? It has to hurt the morale."

"That's for sure. I just wish Coach Glassman could see what's really going on. She's so oblivious!"

Lishia continued her friendly act with Gillian at Allegro's. But when Gillian put two and two together, seeing that Lishia and Riley were actually friends, she turned decidedly frosty toward Lishia. It was like an on-off switch.

"So what's the deal with you, Lishia? Why are you being such a pest?" Gillian questioned as several girls waited to use the ladies' room in the restaurant. "Did you suddenly turn into an adoring cheerleader fan?"

"Huh?" Lishia glanced at Riley with uncertainty. It seemed the jig was up.

"You know," Gillian continued, "like one of those pathetic losers who can't get enough of being around the cheerleaders, so she makes herself a total obnoxious pest?" Gillian laughed loudly, along with a few others, and Lishia felt her cheeks growing warm.

"Be nice," Riley told Gillian.

"I wasn't talking to *you*." Gillian tossed Riley a warning look, then turned back to Lishia. "Seriously, what are you up to anyway?"

"Excuse me," Lishia feigned an apologetic expression. "I didn't know it was such an exclusive club. Am I supposed to apply for membership just to be friends with a cheerleader?"

Someone chortled.

"Of course not." Amanda gave Gillian a questioning look as she stepped up to the mirror by the sinks. "We're not like that at all, Lishia. Don't let Gillian get to you. She's just having an off day."

"And remember that some girls get their kicks by being mean," Riley declared as the line for the toilets moved forward.

"I'm not mean," Gillian shot back at her.

"Hey, I never mentioned names. I merely said *some girls*, but if the shoe fits . . ." Riley shrugged innocently as she went into a bathroom stall.

Gillian rolled her eyes, whispering something to Vanessa as they both giggled, then peered at Lishia as if she were part of a freak show.

"Maybe you should share with the class," Lishia told Gillian.

"I doubt you'd appreciate it," Gillian said.

Lishia's hands balled into fists. What right did Gillian have to go around making other people feel bad? Lishia sniffed the air with a curious expression. "What is that horrid smell?" she asked.

"It's a bathroom," Gillian declared. "What do you think it's supposed to smell like?"

"It smells more like the guys' locker room after a wrestling

44

match." Lishia gave a disgusted face. "Seriously, it smells like really bad BO in here."

Vanessa looked slightly shocked as she hurried into the next available stall, and Amanda giggled as she zipped her bag and stepped away from the mirror.

"Oh, that's just Gillian," Riley called as she emerged from a stall. "Gillian always smells like that after a game or practice. She can't help it."

Lishia feigned a surprised expression. "Oh, I'm sorry." Her hand flew over her mouth. "I didn't mean . . ."

"Yeah, right." Gillian narrowed her eyes, but her cheeks were flushing as if this had embarrassed her. As Lishia took her turn to use a stall, she felt justified, like Gillian had deserved that. She suppressed a tinge of guilt by deciding that it might do Gillian some good to be the one picked on for a change.

"Some people need to get a life," Gillian said as a toilet flushed.

Lishia supposed this was aimed at her but decided to just ignore it. Fortunately, Gillian was nowhere to be seen when Lishia emerged from the stall to wash her hands. Amanda was gone too, but Riley was waiting.

"I think you might've offended Gillian," Riley said in a cautious tone, acting like she had nothing to do with that BO comment.

"Maybe she offended me first," Lishia said defensively.

Riley shrugged as she dried her hands.

"Seriously, where does she get off making others feel bad like that?" Lishia threw her paper towel in the trash.

Riley tipped her head to a stall, probably to indicate Gillian was still here. Lishia shrugged. "I don't care if she hears me. She should know that not everyone wants to bow down and kiss her smelly feet."

Gillian slammed the bathroom stall door with a sour expression. "What is it with you?" She pointed at Lishia. "You're like a pesky mosquito buzzing around my head. I'd like to swat you." She glared at Riley now. "Let me guess, you're involved in this somehow. You want to get back at me for Dayton, but I'm warning you, it's not working."

Riley gave her an innocent look. "I don't have the slightest idea what you're talking about."

"Well, bug off, pest," Gillian snapped at Lishia.

"As far as I know it's still a free country," Lishia tossed over her shoulder as she left with Riley trailing her.

"You were great," Riley assured her once they were out of there. "Very natural."

"Well, she got to me." Lishia still felt anger rising toward Gillian. The weird thing was that she wasn't even sure why. All she knew was that the girl had a way of getting under her skin. Even so, as they walked outside, Lishia was uneasy. Something about that whole exchange felt off—like she had crossed over some invisible line and perhaps she even should apologize to Gillian. But at the same time, she wasn't even sure what she should apologize for. Besides, she didn't want to!

As Riley drove Lishia home, she talked about Gillian, going on and on about what a selfish, skanky, lowlife sort of girl she was and how she really didn't deserve to be on the cheerleading team. "Gillian even slept with Tyler last summer."

"Tyler Braxton?" Lishia asked. "Amanda's boyfriend?"

"Uh-huh." Riley nodded. "Amanda doesn't know, of course."

"Were Amanda and Tyler going out then?"

"Absolutely. Those two have been together for almost a year now. The fact that Gillian would do that—and Amanda is such a good friend to her—well, it's pretty disgusting."

"That's for sure."

"Somehow we've got to bring Gillian down, Lishia. You can see how she's ruining the morale of the entire team with her meanness and bad attitude. Besides that, it's not fair for her to break the rules and get away with it—even if her mom is best friends with the coach. She has to be stopped."

Lishia nodded. She did agree that Gillian needed a good wake-up call. However, Lishia honestly didn't see how she would be able to help with something of that magnitude. Just standing up against Gillian tonight had felt like a hard-fought battle. And Lishia had never been into fighting. She was a peacemaker at heart.

"Next time we go after Gillian, we need to be armed."

"Armed?" Lishia felt a wave of shock and disgust. Surely Riley wasn't thinking of weapons.

"With cameras," she explained. "We need evidence. We need to record Gillian showing her true nature so that Coach Glassman can see it."

"Oh . . . right."

"Tomorrow we'll nail down our plan."

Right now the only plan Lishia wanted to make was to rethink this whole thing with Riley. As much as she wanted Riley for a friend, she knew she was getting in over her head. The sooner she made an escape, the better off she would be. "I'm not so sure I can do that . . . " she began slowly, trying to think of a graceful way to make a break.

"And don't forget—we're invited to Todd Reimer's birthday

party, and it's tomorrow night," Riley said as she pulled up to Lishia's house.

"We?" Lishia tilted her head to one side. "Since when?"

"Didn't you see me talking to Todd tonight? He specifically asked me to invite you."

"Todd Reimer asked you to invite me?" Lishia blinked. Todd was one of the most popular guys in the school. Like many girls, Lishia had nurtured a secret crush on Todd for years.

"Do you think I'm making this up?" Riley sounded hurt.

"No, of course not. I'm just surprised."

"Anyway, the party starts around eight. Maybe you should spend the night at my house afterwards, you know, in case it runs late."

Lishia almost mentioned that it was youth group tomorrow night, but then she remembered her friendless state in youth group recently. Besides that, Riley was talking about Todd Reimer's birthday party—and said Todd wanted Lishia to be there. No way was she going to miss out on this.

"What should I wear?" Lishia asked.

"I know, let's hang together tomorrow afternoon," Riley said. "We can plan what we're wearing to the party and make a really fun day of it. Okay?"

"Sure." Lishia opened the car door. "That sounds awesome. Thanks!" She waved, and as she walked up to her house she realized how close she'd come to giving up on Riley just now. She had almost blown off the friendship! And why? Because she was worried about taking photos of Gillian? Really, when had she turned into such a pathetic little coward? Why shouldn't she be willing to catch Gillian doing something wrong? In a way she'd be doing the whole school a favor. It was wrong for a girl like Gillian to be representing their school as a cheerleader and simultaneously breaking the code of conduct. Why shouldn't Lishia cooperate with Riley in bringing Gillian down? In a way it seemed like a responsibility.

five

"Doesn't Todd remind you of Johnny Depp?" Lishia asked Riley as they were trying on clothes. Riley had declared she had "nothing to wear," and they had headed for the nearest mall to do some last-minute shopping. As usual, Lishia had been stuck looking on the clearance rack, while Riley gathered her selection from the "just arrived" rack. However, as they tried things on, Lishia couldn't see much difference in the items—well, other than the price tags.

"Now that you mention it, yes. He does have that mysterious quality about him." Riley gave a little turn so that the flared skirt she was trying on swirled out.

"Pretty," Lishia approved. "It would look good with that blue top you just tried on."

"And Dayton likes blue."

"Dayton?" Lishia frowned.

"You don't think I'm going to let Gillian walk away with him, do you?" Riley gave a mischievous smile. "Not without a little fight, anyway."

"Really?"

"Sure." Riley nodded. "Dayton still likes me. I just need to remind him of a couple of things. You know, to give him a chance to think this thing over."

"Oh . . . ?"

"It's a free country still . . . right?"

"Of course."

Riley gave her a sly look. "And you do know that Todd is currently between girlfriends, don't you?"

Lishia smiled shyly. "I thought he might be."

"So you need to look your very best for him tonight."

Now Lishia giggled. "Like he'll notice."

"He noticed you last night."

Lishia wasn't sure whether to believe Riley or not. As much as she wanted to believe her, the old adage "if it seems too good to be true, it probably is" was running through her head.

"Come on," Riley urged her, "take some chances. We are only young once, Lishia. You don't have to live like you're an old lady." She pointed to the blouse Lishia was trying on. "And I hate to pick on you, but that makes you look like an old lady." She reached for something from her dressing room. "Here, try this instead. I'm sure that neckline will catch Todd's eye."

Lishia giggled as she took the pale pink shirt into her changing room. She had admired it on Riley, although Riley had claimed the color was wrong. As Lishia tried it on, she thought it actually looked even better on her than on Riley.

"That's perfect," Riley announced when Lishia showed her. "You have to get it."

"It's too much." Lishia frowned at the price tag.

"But it's so perfect!" Riley's brow creased. "You have to get it."

"I can't afford it."

Riley stuck her lower lip out now. "You're no fun!"

"Sorry." Lishia held up her hands. "Unlike some people, I have limited funds." She grimaced at this—she knew she sounded just like her mother. Unfortunately, it was the truth. "But I will get the skirt," she called out as she went back to change into her own clothes.

As they went to the cashier, Riley snatched the pink shirt. "Fine, if you don't want this, I do."

Lishia tried not to feel hurt as she watched Riley place the shirt with her other pieces. Really, why should she care if Riley wanted it? Riley's parents were much better off than Lishia's. Why shouldn't she buy from whichever rack she pleased? Still, it stung.

Then as they were leaving the store, Riley reached into her shopping bag, pulled out the pink shirt, and handed it to Lishia. "Here, this is for you," she declared with a big grin.

"What?"

"It's a gift."

"No way." Lishia shook her head.

"Way!" Riley stuck out her lower lip again. "You really don't want to offend me, do you?"

Lishia looked longingly at the pink shirt. "Not really."

"Good." Riley threw back her head and laughed. "Seriously, what are friends for, anyway?"

"Thanks," Lishia told her. "That was really nice."

Riley paused in front of a hair salon, glancing at her watch. She turned to Lishia. "Do you really want to color your hair?"

Lishia's eyes grew wide. "What do you mean?"

"I mean, we could see if they could fit you in. This is where I get my hair done, and they're really good. Sometimes they take walk-ins, and—"

"But there's no way I can afford that," Lishia said suddenly.

"Come on," Riley urged, "let's just ask. They probably don't have time for you anyway."

The next thing Lishia knew, Riley was standing there talking to the receptionist. As ridiculously impossible as this all seemed, Lishia knew that she really did want to do something different with her hair. Ever since Chelsea had come onto the scene, Lishia had been rethinking her own natural color. Maybe it was true—maybe her auburn hair was mousy . . . maybe blondes really did have more fun.

"They can do it!" Riley exclaimed.

"But I still can't afford—"

"Never mind. I'll put it on my card and you can pay me back later."

"But I can't—"

"Do you want to catch Todd's eye tonight or not?" Riley gave her an impatient look.

"Well, I—"

"If we're going to do this, we need to get moving," the hairdresser urged Lishia.

"Go!" Riley put her hand on Lishia's back as she removed her bags and purse. "Indulge yourself for once!"

Just like that, Lishia was suddenly getting her hair shampooed. Unreal! She tried not to think about things like money and paying Riley back. After all, it wasn't as if Riley gave her a choice in this matter. Besides, the truth was, Lishia wanted this. She wanted it badly! As the hairdresser did her work, Lishia imagined what it would feel like to walk into Todd's birthday party and have him stare at her as if seeing her for the first time. She pictured him coming directly to her, taking her hand in his, asking her to dance . . . and that would be only the beginning!

Todd was just getting down on one knee and asking her to become his wife when the hairdresser proclaimed, "Finished!"

"Huh?" Lishia woke herself from her daydream.

"With just enough time for a cigarette break before my next client." The hairdresser grinned. "What do you think?"

Lishia stared into the mirror. "Wow." Her hand went up to her lightened hair. She looked like someone else. "Is that really me?"

"Pretty chic, eh?"

Lishia wasn't so sure. After years of auburn hair, it was shocking to see herself as a blonde. "I like the cut," she managed to say as she turned her head from side to side, watching the sleek, highlighted hair moving. It was definitely pretty, but she wasn't sure that it was really her. It was like she'd turned into someone else.

"You look fantastic," Riley said as she came over to look.

"Do you really think so?"

"On with you," the hairdresser commanded. "I have to clean up my station now. You'll have to gawk at yourself somewhere else."

"I already took care of the bill," Riley said as she handed Lishia back her things. "And now we have just enough time to get home and get ready for the big night." She shook her head in amazement. "You really look hot, Lishia. Almost like someone else."

"Yeah, that's what worries me." She touched her hair, surprised to find that it even felt different.

"A new and improved you," Riley assured her.

Lishia began to giggle as they walked through the mall. "Is it just my imagination, or am I catching more looks from guys?"

"They're looking at both of us," Riley told her. "With your new 'do, we probably look pretty good together."

"I guess so." Lishia wondered what her mom would say when she saw it. Not that her mother was opposed to such things, but she would question how Lishia could afford it. "I will pay you back," she told Riley, "but it might take a while."

"Don't worry about it . . . I'm not."

❦

Dressed for the party, Lishia wasn't exaggerating when she told Riley that she felt like "a million bucks."

"And you look like it too." Riley seemed slightly troubled. "In fact, now I'm hoping I didn't create a monster. You better not upstage me in front of Dayton. I know he has this twisted notion that he prefers blondes lately."

Lishia laughed lightly. "Don't worry, I'm setting my sights on the birthday boy tonight." She hoped she wasn't going to be in for too much of a disappointment.

"And you're still going to deliver Todd that birthday present we talked about?"

Lishia nodded. "I am."

"Cool." She parked her car along the street, where already dozens of cars were lined up. "And you have my phone, and it's all charged and ready in case you need it, right? And the camcorder too?"

"It's in the bag." Lishia patted the sleek little Kate Spade purse Riley had loaned her for the evening. She didn't want to admit it, but she was feeling a bit like Cinderella tonight. However, she knew that this party was also meant to be a mission. More than anything, Riley wanted Lishia to snag some compromising photos or video footage of Gillian—something they could use as evidence with Mrs. Glassman. Lishia had her doubts as to whether this would really happen, but to appease Riley, who'd been very sweet today, she acted like she was playing along. After all, wasn't that what friends were for?

Lishia felt nervous as they entered the already crowded yard, where kids were milling about and what sounded like a live band was blasting from the backyard. She had no idea what to expect, although she suspected that this was an unchaperoned party and, based on rumors she'd heard in school, those red plastic cups probably contained alcohol. Although she didn't want to admit it (not even to herself), that bothered her some. However, she rationalized, if—and she wasn't even sure she would, but *if*—Riley imbibed, Lishia would simply designate herself as their driver. Under the circumstances, wasn't that the right thing to do?

As she followed Riley inside the house, watching as the confident girl comfortably greeted friends, Lishia could imagine what her mother would say about this. But instead of listening, she blocked it out. After all, she had to grow up someday. This was the norm for most kids. It was about time Lishia experienced it for herself.

Not the drinking part, of course, but she might as well see firsthand what it was all about. Never mind that her old friends would be shocked and appalled if they knew. They were probably all at youth group tonight . . . probably not even missing her. Well, she told herself as she held her head high, imitating Riley's self-assured stride, she was a new person now. Growing up and moving on. Oh, she didn't plan to drink tonight, but there didn't seem to be anything wrong with being here and having a good time.

"Hey, Todd," Riley said pleasantly. "Happy birthday!" She hugged him, then nodded to Lishia. "I brought you a little present."

Lishia felt her cheeks growing warm. Why did Riley have to say that? "Happy birthday," Lishia murmured shyly. But as he embraced her in a warm hug, her confidence grew, and without second-guessing herself, she looked him in the eyes and landed a kiss right smack on his lips. "And that's for your birthday."

He let out a loud whoop of laughter. "Thank you!" Then he leaned down and kissed her again. This time her head began to swim a bit, but she didn't protest as she kissed him back. He slipped his arm around her waist. "I think I'll keep my birthday present handy for the time being," he told her.

She smiled up at him, suppressing the urge to giggle like a six-year-old. She couldn't believe this was really happening. Riley looked almost as shocked as Lishia felt. Then she gave her a sly wink and a thumbs-up.

For a while, Lishia felt like she was on top of the world. At Todd Reimer's side, being admired by him, greeting his friends as if she and Todd had been dating for ages . . . life was good!

"Let's get you something to drink," Todd told her as they walked over to the food and drink area. "What would you like?"

"Do you, uh, how about a Sierra Mist?"

He frowned like he'd misheard her. "Huh?"

"I, uh, I mean, a Coke. I think I'd like a Coke."

A slow grin crossed his face. "And perhaps you'd like a little something in your Coke?"

"Ice?"

He laughed. "Here, let me take care of it." He quietly said something to the guy who was playing bartender, and before she knew it he was handing her what she knew was a Coke spiked with something.

She took a sniff, then shook her head. "I don't drink alcohol."

He looked shocked. "Seriously? Never?"

"Never."

His hand slipped away from where it had been snugly holding on to her waist, and his smile faded. "Oh . . ." He reached for the drink and took a sip with a dismayed expression. "Sorry. I mean, it's not like I put anything illegal in it. Just a little rum is all."

Everything in her wanted to grab the drink back from him. She wanted to tell him she was just kidding and that she loved to drink, that she drank all the time . . . but her lips seemed to be glued tightly together. She watched sadly as he excused himself and went to greet some newcomers. It seemed that her moment in the limelight was over.

"Hey, Lishia," said a guy's voice. "You're looking all right."

She turned to see Dayton studying her closely. "Where's Gillian?" she asked.

He shrugged. "It's not like I keep the girl on a leash. Besides, we're not really going out, you know. Not officially anyway." He moved closer, like he was really checking her out. "You've changed, Lishia." He smiled approvingly.

"It's Riley's influence," she said quickly. Then she smiled. "Remember her? Your ex-girlfriend?"

He grinned sheepishly. "Don't remind me."

"Riley is a really cool girl," Lishia said defensively. "We're becoming good friends, and I'm starting to see there's a lot more to her than I realized."

Dayton looked surprised. "Really?"

"Really. For one thing, she's a loyal friend."

He nodded like he was thinking about that.

"And believe it or not, she's still into *you*." She thumped him on the chest.

Now he looked skeptical. "Tell me another one."

"She is, Dayton. She told me so just today."

"Get out of here." He took a sip from his red plastic cup.

"Seriously, she wishes you guys had never broken up."

"You're full of it."

She looked directly at him. "I swear I'm telling the truth, Dayton."

"Does she know you're talking to me?" he asked quietly.

Lishia glanced around the crowded room. "No."

A slow smile crept onto his face. "So old Riley still has a thing for me?"

Lishia hoped she hadn't made a mess out of this. "I think she does. But I also think you've hurt her, Dayton. It might not be that easy to get her back." She looked over his shoulder to see that Gillian and a couple of her friends had just come into the room. Bad timing.

"What's wrong?" he asked.

"Nothing." She forced a smile and concocted a quick plan. "I just spotted your new girlfriend."

"Huh?"

"You know who."

"Like I said, Gillian and I aren't really together. We went out a couple of times, that's all."

"Then you're not aware that she goes around telling everyone you're madly in love with her?"

"What?" He looked confused.

"Or maybe you are aware? But, seriously, Gillian Rodowski? I'm surprised you'd settle for someone like that." She acted like she wanted to escape now. "Seriously, she's coming this way and I'm so outta here."

"Wait." He put a hand on her arm. "What you said about Ril—"

"Hey, Dayton," Gillian said in a silky voice, linking her arm into his in what was clearly a territorial gesture as she gazed into his eyes. "What's up, my man?"

Dayton looked uneasy, and Lishia tossed him a knowing glance. "See what I mean?" she said quietly.

"What?" Gillian turned to Lishia, then blinked in surprise. "Lishia Vance?"

Lishia smirked. "Gillian Rodowski?"

Gillian reached over and flicked a strand of Lishia's hair. "I see you took my advice and got that dull 'do revived." She laughed in a mean way.

Lishia remembered Riley's list. "Speaking of advice . . ." She sniffed the air, then made a disgusted face. "I hear there's a new deodorant that's guaranteed to tackle the toughest odors. Maybe you should give it a try."

Dayton actually chuckled, and Gillian punched him in the arm.

"Ouch!" He frowned at her. "Take it easy."

"Since we're sharing advice, here's a beauty tip for you . . ." Gillian narrowed her eyes. "I know a plastic surgeon who's a magician at breast implants, and you could certainly use some help in that—"

"Ladies, ladies," Dayton erupted in laughter. "Let's keep this civilized."

"Don't worry," Lishia assured Dayton, then turned to Gillian. "I really can't trust your recommendation of a plastic surgeon"—she pointed at Gillian's face—"seeing how you're still stuck with that nose and all." Now she smiled at Dayton. "I think it's sweet that you're able to overlook that sort of thing." She patted his cheek for drama. "It speaks highly of your character."

Dayton seemed partly stunned and partly amused. Meanwhile, Gillian looked like she wanted to shred Lishia to pieces. Lishia decided not to stick around to find out. She gave them both a little finger wave and turned and walked away—hoping that Gillian didn't have a knife on her. As Lishia made her way across the crowded room, she realized her knees were actually trembling. She couldn't believe what she'd just said, what nerve she'd shown (or was it stupidity?), and all without the aid of alcohol either! She did feel a little uneasy about something . . . something she couldn't really put her finger on . . . or maybe she didn't want to. But Gillian deserved that. She had it coming. And more.

six

s it true?" Riley asked Lishia when they met up again in the backyard. Lishia had slipped out, retreating into the shadows back behind the area where the band was playing. She still couldn't quite believe what she'd done in there, and she wasn't sure she wanted to face Gillian again. Instead she'd found a lawn chair, making herself comfortable while listening to the music, and it turned out the band wasn't too bad.

"Is what true?" She sat up straight and peered at Riley.

"That you and Gillian got into a big fight?"

Lishia shrugged. "Not exactly a big fight."

Riley looked disappointed. "Brandon Procter said it was spectacular."

"Really? Spectacular?" Lishia giggled.

"Brandon is known to exaggerate."

"Well, we did exchange words," Lishia admitted. "It got a little ugly."

"Did you get any photos?"

Lishia frowned. "How was I supposed to get photos when I was in the middle of a conversation? Where were you anyway?"

"Busy." Riley's mouth twisted to one side. "At least you had witnesses."

"And you can be sure I'm on Gillian's most hated list now. She looked like she wanted to kill me."

"Well, you'll never guess what happened after you disappeared."

"What?"

"Dayton publicly dumped Gillian."

"Seriously?"

She nodded. "And he wants to get back with me." She grinned. "But I'm still playing hard to get." Lishia told Riley a bit of what she'd said to Dayton.

"Oh, Lishia, you really are my best friend." Riley threw her arms around her and hugged her tightly. "Thanks!"

"But now I better watch my back when Gillian is around." Lishia glanced over toward the pool area. "Is she still around?"

Riley nodded. "You'd think she'd take a hint, but no, she's still here. Right now she's flirting shamelessly with the birthday boy. Poor Todd."

Lishia rolled her eyes. "Poor Todd?"

"Gillian's had way too much to drink, and she's throwing herself at him."

"Maybe Todd likes that." Lishia was still feeling the sting of his rejection. Just because she wouldn't drink. She'd had a higher opinion of him.

"No, he doesn't like it." Riley reached for the purse. "In fact, I should get some photos of that."

"Have at it," Lishia told her. "But I'm not going back in

there while Gillian's still around. Who knows what she'd do to me while under the influence?"

"But I need your help." Riley reached for her hand and pulled her to her feet.

"What am I—"

"Just continue your conversation," Riley said. "Get Gillian to show her true colors while I've got the camera running. I'm going to pretend to be getting a shot of Todd for his birthday. But you'll bait Gillian, and we'll see what kind of fit she'll throw. If we get lucky, she'll use some bad language." She pointed at Lishia. "And maybe you can mention something about how she's drunk—you know, get her to deny it by saying what she's had to drink. Meanwhile the camera will be rolling."

"You really think you can get away with that?"

"If we stay apart like we originally planned—so she doesn't guess that we're working together on this."

Lishia was already feeling tired of this game. She'd even been feeling guilty for missing youth group tonight. And for what? Todd had quickly grown tired of her. Gillian had turned into a mortal enemy.

"You're the *best* friend," Riley gushed as she gently nudged Lishia with her elbow. "I mean it!" Then she hurried on ahead so it wouldn't look like they were in cahoots. Still, those words warmed Lishia. If nothing else came of tonight, she had shown her loyalty to Riley. And Gillian deserved what she got.

Lishia straightened her spine as she entered the room. Ready for Act Two. She zeroed in on Todd to start with. Just like Riley had said, there was Gillian, draped all over the poor birthday boy. Todd actually looked slightly desperate now, but his friends were just standing around laughing at the spectacle Gillian was making of herself. Lishia walked past Dayton, who was looking on with an interested expression.

"Looks like you escaped her just in time," Lishia said to him as she snatched his drink cup. "Thanks!"

He grinned.

Carrying the cup, which appeared to be half full of beer, she made her way to Todd. She could see Riley nearby and knew this was her one big chance. When she reached Todd, she gave him a curious look, then shook her head as if disappointed. "I thought you had better taste in women," she said as she casually pretended to drink from the half-full cup. Then, making a face, she handed him the cup. "And beer too. What is this cheap stuff, anyway?"

He looked surprised, then amused. "You're right, it is cheap beer," he admitted.

"I thought so." She barely tipped her head toward Gillian, who was glaring at her like she wanted to tear Lishia's hair out by the roots. "But it all seems to add up." She gave Todd a tolerant smile. "Thank you for inviting me to your party. I'd like to say it's been fun, but it hasn't." She turned away.

"Wait!" Todd called out.

Lishia turned back with an innocent look. "What?"

"Don't go yet!" Todd was trying to peel Gillian off of him.

"What're you doing?" Gillian demanded, grabbing onto his arm. "You said you wanted to—"

"Leave me alone," he told her.

"But we were gonna go upstairs," she said pathetically.

"Maybe you should have some coffee," Lishia suggested.

"Maybe you shoul' go an' . . ." Gillian staggered as she narrowed her eyes and spewed out some bad language.

"Really?" Lishia feigned shock. "I'm sure you wouldn't talk like that if you weren't drunk, Gillian." She resisted the urge to make sure Riley was getting this all on camera.

"I'm not drunk," Gillian slurred.

Lishia pointed to the drink in Gillian's hand. "What is that, like your fifth drink?"

"You don' know what you're talkin' 'bout. I can hold my liquor, you little shlut!" She staggered toward Lishia, letting loose with some really off-color words as well as personal threats.

"I know you don't mean that," Lishia said as she cautiously stepped back. "That's just the alcohol talking. You really should consider a treatment program. I think you might need professional help."

Gillian made a sloppy lunge toward Lishia, but Todd and a couple of his friends blocked her as she sputtered and swore, spilling her drink all over them.

"Somebody needs a little time-out," Lishia said, and several of them laughed.

"Or maybe a little dunk in the pool," Brandon Procter yelled. "That'd cool her off." Just like that, several of the guys hoisted Gillian up and carried her, kicking and screaming, out to the pool, where they heaved her into the water with a big splash, followed by roars of laughter and clapping. Riley was getting the whole thing on the camcorder, and everyone was acting like this was the best entertainment ever.

However, Lishia actually felt sorry for Gillian as she floundered in the water. She was also worried that in her drunken state, Gillian might actually drown and even suggested someone help her out. But the cold water must've sobered her up some, and Gillian managed to claw her way out. Dripping and angry, she pointed at Lishia. "You are dead meat!" she yelled.

"Come on," Todd said as he grabbed Lishia by the arm. "Let's get you away from her before there's bloodshed."

With the sounds of Gillian screaming horrible threats behind them, Lishia let Todd lead her through the house, down a hallway, and up some stairs until they wound up in what appeared to be the rather luxurious master bedroom suite. "Is this your parents' room?" she asked as he closed and locked the door.

"Yes." He nodded. "But she won't find us here."

Lishia looked around the elegant-looking room and shook her head. "That's right, she won't." She turned for the door, ready to make her getaway.

"You're not going back out there, are you?" He looked alarmed.

Lishia managed to laugh. "Well, it might be safer than in here with you."

He laughed. "Do you seriously think I'd try to get you into my *parents'* bed?" He made a disgusted face. "Gross!"

"It does seem a little creepy."

"You got that right." He pointed to a pair of easy chairs by a set of French doors. "Want to sit and talk?"

"Sure," she agreed. "In fact, I'd like to ask you some questions."

"Questions?"

She nodded as she sat down. "For starters, where are your parents?"

He chuckled. "Vegas, baby."

"They went to Vegas on your birthday?"

"It's not actually my birthday until Wednesday."

"Oh, you decided to celebrate early."

He nodded. "You only turn eighteen once. I wanted to do it up big."

"Do your parents know you're having this party?"

He shrugged. "They probably have an idea . . . and the neighbors will tell them."

She couldn't believe how nonchalant he was. "And you won't get in trouble?"

"Everything will be all back together by the time they get home Sunday night. I put away everything that's breakable. And I have a cleaning service all lined up for tomorrow morning."

"Really?"

He nodded. "My older brothers used to do the same thing."

"So you're just following their example."

He shrugged.

"And are you having a good birthday party?"

He grinned. "I am now."

She smiled and relaxed a little. "Well, thanks for saving me from Gillian."

He slowly shook his head. "If I were you, I'd watch out for that girl. She looked like she wanted to put you six feet under, and I doubt that she'll cool off too easily."

"Kind of unbecoming for a cheerleader."

He laughed. "I've seen worse."

"Really?" She leaned forward. "Tell me more."

He began relaying some other crazy stories about cheerleaders. Even Riley had pulled some embarrassing stunts. "They're only human," he said finally. "Just like all of us." He pointed to her. "Except for you. You seem to have some kind of superiority complex. Like you really think you're better than the rest of us. What's up with that?"

Lishia took in a slow breath as a small wave of guilt washed over her. What was the goody-goody "Christian" girl doing at a party like this? Really, who was she trying to fool?

"You got to ask me your questions," he said. "Now I want to know what you're up to. Why are you here tonight?"

"To celebrate with you." She used a big smile to cover her anxious feelings. Why shouldn't she be here? Except that her conscience was trying to get the best of her. The problem with a conscience was that it could be a pest sometimes. Like it had a mind of its own. Maybe the only choice was to simply block it out. That's what she would do.

"So why did you go after Gillian like that?" he persisted. "And why did you act like you don't drink and then complain about the quality of my beer, which I do admit is substandard?"

"I could tell you the truth"—she smiled slyly—"but then I'd have to kill you."

He laughed.

"And that would be a shame to do at your birthday party."

Todd peeked out the window—then swore. "The cops!"

"No way." Lishia felt sick with fear as she stood.

"Come on." He grabbed her hand and turned off the light. "Out here." He led her out the French doors and onto the terrace. Then, after helping her climb over a railing, he guided her onto a low, sloped roof. They both climbed down a trellis, and with him holding her hand, they streaked across a dark side yard, through an opening in the hedge, and out onto the dark street.

"Just keep walking like we're out for a nice evening stroll," he calmly told her as he continued to hold her hand. "No big deal."

"Works for me," she said in relief. Her heart was still pounding, but the truth was, this was the most fun she'd had all night.

"Are you hungry?" he asked when they reached a corner with a bus stop.

"Come to think of it, I am."

So they waited for the bus, rode it into town, and ordered a late dinner at a little Mexican café. Lishia couldn't believe how relaxed she felt around Todd now. It was as if they'd been friends for ages. Maybe that happens when you elude the police together. She shuddered to think of the trouble she'd narrowly avoided tonight. But then, like she was getting so good at, she decided to block that out too. *Stay in the moment*, she told herself. *Enjoy this!* So she did, eating and laughing and making jokes about the party getting crashed by the cops.

"Okay, tell me the truth," she said finally. "Isn't this better than getting totally wasted and watching all your friends acting like idiots?" She stuck her spoon into the custard flan they were sharing for dessert and smiled.

He nodded. "Now I just have to think of some kind of explanation for the cops. I'm sure they'll want to question me . . . eventually."

"You could always tell them that it was a *surprise* party," she teased.

"That's it!" he declared. "You're a genius, Lishia. I'll say it was a surprise party, and when I saw it was getting out of control, I decided to split."

"You're really going to lie to the police?" She tried to conceal her disappointment. After all, she'd practically suggested it. Still, she had this old-fashioned longing for Todd to be a stand-up kind of guy, to own up to his mistakes. Of course, that would get him into trouble. Might even get her into trouble. Perhaps he was right.

"It's not completely a lie," he said. "I mean, it was originally going to be a surprise party. It was actually Tyler and Dayton's idea to throw this little gig in the first place. When they heard my folks were out of town, they decided to do it at my place. I went along with it."

She nodded.

"And who knows, maybe the cops won't ask. Especially since I'm nowhere to be found."

Lishia tried to appear in agreement, but some of the magic was wearing off. Not only that, but now she remembered that she was supposed to spend the night at Riley's house. But what if Riley was in jail now? Where would she stay? What would she tell her parents if she had to come home? She decided to try Riley's cell.

"Hey," Riley said cheerfully, like nothing was wrong.

"Did you get busted?"

Riley laughed. "Nah. Dayton and I made our exit long before the cops arrived. Then I drove him over to my place. We've been hanging here while my parents are still at their movie. What about you? Are you in jail?"

"No, of course not." Lishia shuddered to imagine how that would've felt—to be making a phone call from the police station. She didn't even want to think about it. Instead she explained how they'd gotten away and where she and Todd had landed, and the four agreed to meet up at Riley's, where Riley said they'd continue to party. Lishia wasn't too sure what she thought about that idea, but shortly after they arrived, Riley's parents got home, and it seemed a good time for the guys to call it a night.

"What a bizarre evening," Lishia told Riley after they were back in her bedroom. "At first I was scared to death I was going to get taken to jail and my parents would kill me. But then it's like everything turned completely around and Todd and I ended up having a really great time."

"Life's funny." Riley was flipping through DVDs.

"But seriously, if Todd hadn't looked out the window just when he did . . . we'd have been toast." She shook her head. "I can't even imagine how I would've explained it to my parents. Do you think other kids got arrested?"

"Probably."

"Like Gillian?"

"I hope so." Riley gave a mischievous smile. "Then I wouldn't even need to show Mrs. Glassman my evidence."

"How did you and Dayton know to get away?"

Now Riley got a funny look, like there was something she was holding back . . . some information she was keeping.

"Did someone tip you off?" Lishia asked curiously.

"Not exactly."

"How then?"

Riley narrowed her eyes. "Do you swear you'll never tell a soul?"

Lishia blinked. "Uh . . . okay."

"I'm the one who called the police."

"No way!"

Riley suppressed giggles. "Uh-huh."

"How is that possible?"

Riley explained how she and Dayton left the party and drove into town, where she used a pay phone and tipped off the police anonymously.

"I can't believe you'd do that! What were you thinking?"

Lishia demanded. "You knew I was still there! I could've gotten—"

"I knew you were with Todd, and I knew he'd get you out safely, Lishia. Lighten up, okay?"

"How could you possibly know that?"

"Because he's Todd, and it's his house. Of course he'd have a backup plan. And I was right. He did. And you already told me you had the best time with him. So, really, instead of being mad, you should thank me."

Lishia did not feel like thanking Riley. "You could've gotten me arrested."

"But I didn't." Riley made a pouty face. "I can't believe you're getting mad. Especially when I think of all I've done for you."

"What?" Lishia folded her arms across her front.

"First I helped you and Todd get together, right?"

Lishia shrugged, then nodded.

"But even better, I've secured you a position on the cheerleading squad."

Lishia looked skeptical.

"You know Gillian will get suspended if she's been arrested."

"Maybe she got away too."

"She was too wasted to get away." Riley firmly shook her head. "No, I'm sure she's been arrested and booked down at city hall. And when they check her alcohol level, she'll be in serious trouble. But even if she didn't get arrested, I've got enough on my camcorder to cinch the whole thing. She is definitely history when it comes to cheerleading."

"You're sure about that?"

She reapplied her lip gloss with a smug expression. "So instead of being so mad, you should thank me."

Lishia didn't know what to say.

"Look, I'm sorry I had to put you in harm's way for a little bit," Riley conceded. "But you weren't even drinking, Lishia. You didn't break the law, so you couldn't have gotten into trouble. Don't you get that?"

"I guess so."

"I had to do this for your own good. And for the good of the cheerleading squad. Gillian was bringing us down. Now she'll be out. Can't you see this is something to celebrate?"

"I guess so." But even as she said this, Lishia wasn't so sure. Something about the whole evening felt off to her. The old Lishia would've been appalled at what had transpired . . . the new Lishia was simply dazed and confused.

"Tomorrow we'll start going over the routines," Riley told her. "We've got to get you into tip-top shape before the basketball games begin." Riley stood up and started to teach her a yell, forcing Lishia to make an attempt to go through the motions until she finally blew it so badly that they both collapsed to the floor in giggles. It was hard to stay mad at Riley for long.

seven

Riley spent most of Sunday teaching Lishia routines and texting friends to see who'd gotten in trouble last night. "This is perfect!" she exclaimed as she held her phone in the air.

Lishia threw the pom-poms she'd been borrowing onto the floor, then turned down the music and collapsed onto the sofa. She was ready for a break. "What is it?"

"Gillian got arrested last night."

"Uh-huh . . ." Lishia shrugged. "But that's what you expected would happen."

"But listen to this." Riley went over to check the basement stairs, making sure the door was closed. "Gillian was found by the police in one of the bedrooms, and she was stark naked!"

"Huh?" Lishia sat up straight. "You gotta be kidding."

"Remember she'd been thrown in the pool?"

"Oh, yeah."

"She must've been getting out of her wet clothes. Anyway,

Vanessa says they checked her alcohol level, and it was probably high since Gillian was totally wasted. Any way you look at it, Gillian is in big trouble!" She gave Lishia a high five. "Now back to work!"

Lishia let out a groan. "I'm tired."

"You need to be ready to take Gillian's place—and don't forget we have regionals right after Christmas. Last year we took fifth, and we're determined to do better this year, maybe even qualify for state."

Lishia felt slightly sickened by this thought. It was one thing to replace Gillian, but the idea of competing at the state level was overwhelming. Was she really up to this?

Finally it was getting late in the afternoon, and Lishia knew she should go home. "I have homework," she explained as she started to gather her things. "And you don't want me to ruin my grades before I even have a chance to replace Gillian."

"Good point." Riley patted her on the back. "But then you've always been more academic than me. We probably don't need to worry about your grades."

"Except that I'm taking harder classes," Lishia pointed out, "including some AP ones."

"Maybe you should drop those, you know, just to protect your GPA."

Lishia frowned as she shoved some clothes into her duffle bag. She didn't want to drop her classes.

"Anyway, think about it," Riley said as they went to the car. "We need committed cheerleaders."

Or cheerleaders who need to be committed, Lishia thought wryly. Really, was she ready to obsess over this? Did she have a choice? However, she kept her thoughts to herself as Riley drove her home. "Thanks for everything," she told Riley as she got out of the car.

"Thank you!" Riley grinned. "I can't wait to see Gillian's face tomorrow."

Lishia nodded, but as she went into her house an image of Gillian's enraged face flashed through her imagination. The last time she'd seen her, Gillian had looked like she wanted to kill Lishia. Hopefully, she'd cool off by Monday.

"What on earth happened to you?" Mom demanded as Lishia came into the kitchen.

"Huh?" Lishia tried not to look guilty as she opened the fridge and foraged through the fruit drawer, finally removing an apple. What had Mom heard about last night?

"Look at me, Lishia," Mom demanded.

Bracing herself, Lishia turned to face her mom. "What do you mean?"

Mom pointed at her head. "Your hair! Your beautiful auburn hair."

Lishia touched her hair. "Oh, that."

"Oh, *that*?" Mom's eyebrows shot up. "What on earth did you do to it?"

"It's just hair, Mom." Lishia let exasperation seep into her voice. "It's not like I went out and got a tattoo."

"But why would you do that? Your hair was gorgeous. Everyone said so, honey." Mom frowned, then shook her head. "I don't understand."

"I wanted a new look," Lishia explained.

"But you don't look like yourself."

"I'm still me, Mom." Lishia took a big bite out of the apple and rolled her eyes.

"Did you and Riley go to church today?" Mom looked suspicious.

Now Lishia realized she needed to handle this more gently. "Riley isn't really into church anymore."

"She doesn't go to church?" Mom frowned.

"Not since middle school." Lishia sighed. "But I'm hoping I'll be a good influence on her. Maybe I can talk her into going to youth group or something."

Mom looked brighter. "Yes, that's a wonderful idea. You can use your influence to get Riley to go back to church."

"Uh-huh." Lishia took another bite of the apple.

Mom looked slightly concerned now. "Just make sure Riley's not influencing you more than you're influencing her, Lishia." She reached over and touched Lishia's hair, then frowned again. "Your hair was so pretty before. I don't understand why all you girls think you have to become blondes. Really, they're becoming a dime a dozen. In my opinion, they look cheap."

"Thanks a lot, Mom."

"Sorry, honey. Just speaking my mind. You're still a pretty girl." She cocked her head to one side. "But come to think of it, I'm guessing it wasn't cheap. How on earth did you pay for it?"

"Riley paid."

"*What?*" Mom looked mad.

"I'm going to pay her back." Lishia picked up her bag, trying to make her exit.

"Oh, Lishia!"

"I've got homework, Mom." Lishia kept going, ignoring Mom's continued blabbing on about money and debt and how she expected more from Lishia—blah, blah, blah. Seriously, did Mom honestly think that her lectures worked? Or maybe she didn't care—it was simply a form of punishment in itself.

Not for the first time, Lishia wished she wasn't an only child. If there were a few siblings around, her parents might be forced to share the "loving discipline" a bit more. As it was, Lishia usually got all of their parental attention lavished onto her.

❦

News of the birthday party bust was all over the school on Monday. As far as Lishia could tell, the rumors about Gillian getting caught in the buff and arrested were true too. "How did you fare?" Lishia asked Todd when he caught up with her on her way into the cafeteria.

"I had to answer some questions on Sunday morning," he quietly told her. "They stopped by my house just as the cleaners arrived."

Lishia giggled. "How did you explain that?"

"I acted like I was really miffed, like I couldn't believe my friends would actually do this to me. I told them that I'd spent the night at Dayton's, which was true. They knew I wasn't home since they'd checked my house several times throughout the night."

"Seriously?"

"That's what they said."

"But didn't they still suspect you had something to do with it?"

"Sure. But I used your line."

"My line?"

"About the *surprise* party."

"Oh, dear." She shook her head as she picked up a tray.

"They pushed me for names, but I played dumb. I mean, hey, it was a surprise party—how was I supposed to know who did what?"

"And they bought that?"

"Wasn't much else they could do."

"You are one smooth operator, Todd." She placed a salad on her tray.

"Don't look now, but you are being watched," he whispered in her ear.

"Huh?"

His eyes darted to the left and back.

Following his gaze, she spotted Gillian glaring directly at her. "Uh-oh." Lishia gave Todd a worried look.

"Don't worry, I'll protect you," he teased.

"I'll take you up on that," she said as she waited for him to get his cheeseburger. No way was she leaving his side now. They got in line for the cashier, and trying not to be obvious, she sneaked a couple of peeks at Gillian, who was now getting her own lunch. Maybe Lishia had imagined the dagger looks. Just the same, she stayed close to Todd as they joined Riley and Dayton and several others at what Lishia used to consider the "popular" table. Oh, she never would've used that term out loud—it would only classify her as lame. But in her mind, that's what it was. And to be welcome here today, to be sitting with Todd, well, it was almost too much to absorb.

"Hey, there's the birthday boy," someone called from the end of the table. "Did you spend the night in jail too?"

"No way." He laughed.

"But did you hear about Gillian?" Riley said, probably to deflect attention from the kids who escaped the police on Saturday. Everyone was all ears as Riley and a couple other girls relayed the whole incident of Gillian being wasted and naked and how there was a discipline meeting scheduled for after school.

"She's getting suspended from cheerleading," Vanessa said.

"We don't know that for sure," Amanda corrected. "Don't forget this is America and you're innocent until proven guilty."

"Oh, she's guilty, all right," Vanessa declared. "It's all on record down at city hall. I'm telling you, the girl is toast. I'm just thankful I got out of there before it was too late."

"I'm glad I didn't go," Amanda admitted.

"Gillian was a fool to get caught like that," Vanessa said. "But now she's ruined it for our cheerleaders. Thanks to her, we won't have a chance at regionals this year."

Lishia couldn't believe how quickly Vanessa had turned on her friend. Just days ago, those two were inseparable. Now Gillian was sitting by herself on the fringe of the cafeteria. Lishia wasn't sure if this was Gillian's choice—and she couldn't blame her—or if her friends were simply freezing her out. But it was strange to think that last week Riley had been the castoff, and now it was Gillian. What a fickle crowd. But then Lishia remembered her own so-called friends. Glancing toward their regular table, she realized that some of them were actually looking at her with curious expressions. Of course, they would wonder what turn of events had landed her here. She suppressed the urge to laugh, then turned back to the conversation at her table.

"So much for our dreams of getting to state too," Riley said sadly—and believably too. "There's no way we can get it together now."

"Don't give up yet," Amanda told them. "We'll still have a few weeks to break someone in."

"Only if Glassman deals with this quickly," Vanessa said. "Don't forget that this week is Thanksgiving, which means no school for several days—maybe a whole week of lost practices."

"That's right." Amanda started counting the days on her fingers. "We need to push Mrs. Glassman to make her decision right away." She looked at the other cheerleaders. "Now, I know some of you were at the party. Is there any chance anyone else can get suspended too? Be honest."

"Thanks to Riley, I got out of there." Krista smiled at Riley. "Thanks."

"Then Krista texted me," another girl said.

"So Gillian really is the only one going down." Amanda's brow creased. "Well, maybe if we all petition Mrs. Glassman, she'll figure this mess out in a hurry. Because it's not fair to punish the whole team for one person."

Lishia poked at her salad, trying to look disinterested in this conversation where she actually had so much at stake. She couldn't believe how coolly Riley handled it, never once alluding to having had anything to do with anything. It all made Lishia uncomfortable, and every bite of salad landed like stones in her stomach. She was so relieved when lunch was over.

"Wait for me in the girls' locker room after school," Riley told Lishia as they were leaving the cafeteria. "I have that meeting with Glassman."

Lishia agreed, then hurried on to her class. Her biggest fear today was running into Gillian—alone. She had no idea what Gillian would do, if anything, but the looks she'd been throwing Lishia's way were unnerving. By the end of the day, Lishia's imagination was running wild, so much so that she decided not to wait in the girls' locker room. She might run into Gillian in there. Instead, she texted Riley and hung out in the library.

"There you are," Riley said when she found Lishia doing homework. "Didn't you get my messages?"

Lishia blinked. "No. This is a library—my phone's turned off."

"Well, come with me."

"Huh?"

"We need your testimony."

"My testimony?" Lishia remembered giving her Christian testimony at a retreat once—surely Riley didn't mean that.

"About what Gillian said and did to you."

"Huh?"

"I showed Glassman part of the video of Gillian at the party. Now Glassman wants to hear what you have to say." Riley was tugging her down the hall, toward the gym. "You need to tell the truth, but make it sound innocent."

"I am innocent," Lishia said. At least she thought she was innocent . . . or sort of.

"Explain how Gillian took a dislike to you—probably because you're my friend. Tell Glassman about how Gillian picked on you Friday night. Remember the scene at the restaurant? Anyway, just tell her—in a nice, polite way—how Gillian raged at you at the party. Also be sure to mention you weren't drinking. We're all saying that we thought it was a regular birthday party, and when we realized alcohol was being served, we left. That's why none of us—besides Gillian—got in trouble. Okay?" She was opening the door to the locker room.

"Okay . . . ?" Lishia was unsure, and now her stomach felt like there was a brick in the bottom of it.

"Here she is," Riley announced as she pulled Lishia toward Mrs. Glassman's office.

"Have a seat," Mrs. Glassman told her in a serious tone.

Lishia nodded without speaking and sat down.

"No need to be nervous. I just have a few questions." She looked at Riley. "You can wait out there. Close the door on your way out."

"I'm sure you know why you're here," Mrs. Glassman began. "Unfortunately, we have to make a decision—and, of course, it's not an easy one."

Lishia nodded again, swallowing hard. "I can imagine."

"So, tell me, were you at the infamous birthday party?"

Lishia was pretty sure that Mrs. Glassman already knew this answer, but she explained anyway, saying how she went there with Riley.

"And did you know there would be alcohol?"

"No," Lishia said quickly. "I, uh, I don't even drink."

"Really?" Mrs. Glassman peered curiously at her.

"Honestly, I don't drink. I think it's dumb. I mean, look what happened to Gillian. I would die if that—" She stopped herself. "Sorry."

"So, speaking of Gillian, I saw Riley's home movie, and you were in it. Care to explain what you did to get Gillian so angry at you?"

Lishia thought hard. "I'm not sure why she was so mad at me, but it probably had to do with what I said to Dayton. There was kind of a love triangle between him and Gillian and Riley. I simply told him that I thought Riley was a better choice." She shrugged. "If you'd seen how Gillian had been acting, you'd probably understand."

"I am disappointed in Gillian," Mrs. Glassman admitted. "But as I told the other girls, I realize that Gillian's family is going through some difficult times, and a part of me understands how that can take a toll on a girl."

Lishia frowned. "I didn't know that."

"No, I'm sure Gillian wouldn't tell you. And really, it's no excuse. The code of conduct still applies." Now Mrs. Glassman asked Lishia some specific questions about the party, including whether she'd seen the other cheerleaders drinking. Fortunately, Lishia hadn't specifically noticed, so she could answer honestly. "Okay, that's all I need," Mrs. Glassman said in a somber tone. "Thank you for your time."

Lishia stood, then paused. "I wish I'd known that Gillian was having problems at home," she said wistfully. "I would've tried to be nicer to her."

Mrs. Glassman shook her head. "Maybe you'll keep that in mind for the future. My hope would be that all you girls would learn a lesson from this—and be smarter next time."

Lishia nodded as she left. A lesson . . . had she learned a lesson yet? If so, what was it? Or perhaps there was still a lesson to come. Mostly she was glad to have that little interrogation behind her.

eight

"What is going on with you?" Megan Bernard asked Lishia the next day as they walked into their AP history class.

"Huh?" Lishia looked blankly at Megan.

"It's like you turned into someone else overnight."

"Overnight?" Lishia tipped her head to the side. "You mean *last* night?"

"You know what I mean. Last week you were one person, and now you're someone else."

Lishia looked down at herself, then shook her head. "Nope, you're wrong. I'm the same person."

"You've changed."

"Hey, change is good." Lishia took a seat in back, and Megan sat next to her.

"First you started by shoving your old friends away," Megan challenged.

"I never shoved anyone away," Lishia defended herself.

"You kept us all at arm's length."

Lishia shrugged. "I think it was mutual."

"Anyway, now you've gone and changed your hair and your friends, and we heard you went to a drinking party."

"A drinking party?" Lishia chuckled.

"You know what I mean." Now Megan smiled. "The only reason I'm telling you this is because we care about you. As your Christian brothers and sisters, we want to warn you that you're going down a bad road."

Lishia frowned. "How do you know what kind of road I'm on?"

"We can see it. You're hanging with the wrong crowd, acting like someone else. And you didn't even go to youth group on Saturday."

"What are you, the church police?"

"I just happen to care about you." Megan pursed her lips.

"Thanks for caring." Lishia gave her a stiff smile. "But I'm just fine, thank you very much."

"But you should know that Riley is bad news," Megan persisted.

"Are you going to start gossiping about my friend now?" Lishia gave her a disapproving look. "You know what the Bible says about gossip, don't you?"

Megan looked perplexed. Fortunately, their teacher was making his way to the front of the room, and Lishia had an excuse to turn her attention from Megan. She was only partially surprised that Megan had said something like that to her. For starters, their youth pastor was always encouraging kids to hold each other accountable, to keep them from going astray. Besides that, Megan had a reputation for sticking her nose into other people's business.

Lishia decided to simply chalk it up to old-fashioned jealousy. Megan's older sister Bethany had been a lot more popular than Megan. It made sense that Megan might want that too. But it was wrong for her to attempt to make Lishia feel guilty for befriending Riley. Seriously, didn't Megan have any understanding of Christian love? She would be singing a different song when Lishia brought Riley to church with her. It could happen.

By Wednesday, the decision was made. Gillian was suspended indefinitely from cheerleading. And once again, Lishia's presence was requested in Mrs. Glassman's office. Riley had prepared Lishia for this possibility. "You must act totally surprised when she tells you that you're the alternate and offers you a position on the squad," she warned. "There's no way you knew this could happen to you—you are dumbfounded. It might even be impressive if you shed some tears. And be sure to show sympathy for Gillian's loss. After all, her mother is Mrs. Glassman's good friend."

Naturally, Lishia did all of that, including crying. Whether her tears were from joy, relief, fear, or even guilt was unclear, but they were real just the same.

"Here's the list of things you'll need to get." Mrs. Glassman handed her a sheet of paper. "Unfortunately, there's nothing left in the team funds to help you with your uniform now. I suppose you could ask Gillian about selling some of her things and try to get some alterations done . . ."

Lishia grimaced. "I don't know if I could do that."

"Yeah, it might just make her feel worse. Poor Gillian, she's pretty broken up over this."

Lishia glanced down at the list, surprised it was so long.

"As you can imagine, the girls want you to join them in practice immediately." Mrs. Glassman stood. "So get dressed down and meet us in the girls' gym."

Lishia nodded and blew her nose, thanking Mrs. Glass-man. But her heart was still pounding as she pulled on shorts and a tank and tied up her shoes. She knew she should be happy—most girls would be over the moon by now. Really, it was amazing that this was happening to her. She just hoped she was up for it—and that she wouldn't blow it.

More than ever she was grateful for all the time Riley had spent with her, teaching her the routines so she wouldn't look like a total clown when she joined the team. There was no way she had the routines down pat, but at least it would shorten her learning curve. Now she had to be careful not to act like she was picking up on things too quickly. It felt like a balancing act.

As Lishia walked to the girls' gym, she looked forward to when she would no longer be acting—when she could return to responding normally and not feel so guarded about every-thing she said or did. But for the time being she knew there was no room for slipups. She had to continue this charade that she and Riley had so painstakingly created.

She was welcomed to the gym with warm congratulations as well as some slightly suspicious looks. Some girls obvi-ously had trouble believing it was a coincidence that Lishia and Riley had just happened to become best friends—and now this. But as they worked together and Lishia took spe-cial care to be extra nice to everyone, things seemed to settle down.

"We need to practice during Thanksgiving break," Amanda announced when they were back in the locker room. The team agreed to some time slots and locations, and then everyone told each other to have a happy Thanksgiving and went their separate ways.

"You were perfect," Riley told Lishia as they went to her car. "Everyone bought your Oscar-worthy performance."

Lishia let out a weary sigh. "I'll be glad when things settle down. I had no idea how much work it is to be an actress. It's no wonder I took art instead of drama."

Riley laughed. "Well, you pulled this one off like a natural."

Lishia knew that was meant to be a compliment, but somehow she heard it another way—almost as if Riley was praising her for being a good con artist. Anyway, it rubbed her the wrong way, and suddenly Lishia didn't feel like talking. She got out the list that Mrs. Glassman had given her and began to study it.

"Is that the uniform list?" Riley asked as she stopped for the light.

"Uh-huh . . ." Lishia sighed. "Wow, I had no idea everything was this expensive."

"Yeah. And it's too late for you to participate in the fundraisers."

"I don't know if I can afford this." Lishia looked at Riley with worried eyes. The truth was, she knew she could not afford this. No way, no how. "Maybe this was all a mistake and I should just—"

"No! You have to do this, Lishia," Riley insisted. "We'll figure out a way to make it work."

"Mrs. Glassman suggested I might buy stuff from Gillian."

"Ugh, you don't want her things. Even if she was willing, which I doubt, there'd be no way to know how she might sabotage them before she handed them over."

"But everything costs so much." Lishia folded the papers and tucked them back into her bag.

"Don't start freaking yet. The first game isn't for a couple of weeks. We'll think of something by then."

"Like rob a bank?"

Riley laughed.

"I don't know . . ." Lishia felt close to tears now. "Maybe this really was a mistake. Maybe this is what I get for being underhanded."

"Don't say that. You weren't underhanded."

Lishia bit her lip.

"Gillian brought it all on herself."

"We helped," Lishia quietly admitted.

"All we did was report on what happened."

"Not everything."

"What do you mean?" Riley's brow creased.

"I never told Mrs. Glassman that you and the other cheerleaders there were drinking that night too."

"Well, of course not."

Lishia looked down at the bag in her lap.

"But none of us took it as far as Gillian did either. We didn't make total fools of ourselves."

"Did you know that Gillian's parents were having some problems?" Lishia said quietly.

"Oh, good grief! Everyone's parents have problems. It's no excuse to go to pieces."

"Mine don't."

"Your parents have *no* problems . . . *right*?"

"Nothing big enough to make me go out drinking."

"Then don't. No one expects you to. But don't start feeling all sorry for Gillian either. What's done is done, and for you to turn into a bleeding heart will not help anyone. Not you or Gillian. Do you seriously think she wants your pity now? It's not like it'll undo her suspension."

Lishia knew this was true, but she felt sorry for Gillian just the same.

"Anyway, don't get all bummed about the cost of the outfits," Riley said as she pulled in front of Lishia's house. "We'll figure out something. Maybe we can have a fundraiser just for you."

Lishia nodded. "Thanks."

"Happy Thanksgiving," Riley called out cheerfully.

Lishia returned the greeting with a little less cheer, then hurried into the house to avoid the raindrops that were starting to splatter down. She knew her mom was home because her car was in the driveway. That was the problem with her teaching only half days—she was usually home in the afternoon. Lishia had liked that when she was younger, but sometimes, like today, she would've happily avoided her mom's inquisition about her day.

"Just who I wanted to see," Mom called from the kitchen. "I could use a hand, Lish."

Lishia hesitantly peeked in. "Yeah?"

"Want to help me get the rest of the groceries out of the car?"

"Okay." Lishia pulled her parka back on. At least this bought her a couple of minutes to figure out how to hit Mom with her latest news. She knew she should act like she was excited and happy—but she was so tired of acting. She gathered up the remaining bags, then hurried back inside, dumping them on the counters. "What is all this?" she asked.

"We're hosting Thanksgiving, remember?" Mom shoved a bag of apples into the fridge. "Grandma Willis is coming and—"

"I have some interesting news," Lishia said suddenly.

"What?" Mom paused and looked at her.

"I made the cheerleading squad."

"What?" Mom set a can of cranberry sauce on the counter and gave her a puzzled look. So Lishia explained about a girl getting kicked off. "The routines are all designed for seven girls. It turns out I'm the alternate, so I'll be cheering for basketball season."

Mom broke into a wide smile. "Well, that's wonderful, sweetie. I'm so happy for you. How exciting." Her smile faded. "But you don't seem happy. What's wrong?"

Lishia felt a lump growing in her throat. "I—uh—I'm happy. It's just that—" Now she started to cry.

"What is it?" Mom put her arms around her and hugged her tightly. "Talk to me."

Suddenly Lishia was worried. She wanted to tell her mom everything, but that would get everyone, including her, into trouble. Besides, even if she spilled the beans, how would they possibly untangle everything? What good would come of it? Riley was right—what was done was done.

"Come on, sweetie, tell me what's wrong," Mom urged as she held Lishia at arm's length and looked into her eyes. "You should be dancing for joy—not crying."

"It's just that"—Lishia reached for her bag and pulled out the paperwork—"it costs too much. I can't do it. I'll have to tell them that—"

"Wait a minute." Mom took the papers from her. "Let's see." She began to go over the list, reading it out loud and letting out short exclamations as she read prices. "Oh, my! I had no idea these things were so costly. How did the other girls afford it?"

Lishia explained about fundraisers. "But now it's too late."

"Oh . . ." She handed the list back to Lishia.

"So I should tell them no, huh?" Lishia hoped beyond hope that Mom would agree. Oh, she'd be sad and say it was too bad, but then she'd turn parental and say the wise thing to do at this point was to pass. Lishia could act slightly hurt by this . . . but then she'd agree.

"What about the girl who got suspended?" Mom questioned. "Couldn't you buy her uniform and things from her—at a discount, of course? Or maybe she's the wrong size."

"She's actually about the same size as me . . . well, I don't know about shoes, but I don't want—"

"Well, we could certainly afford new shoes, Lishia. But if you could talk to her and find out if she's—"

"That's just it. She's so mad . . . you know, about getting kicked off . . . I doubt she'll even speak to me." That was an understatement. Gillian would probably claw Lishia's eyes out before she'd let her have her uniform.

"Oh . . . I can see how that might be awkward." Mom nodded. "And I can imagine she must be hurting."

Now Lishia explained that she'd been having problems at home too. "Maybe that's why she was drinking so much that night."

"That's sad." Mom shook her head.

"So I guess I should tell them I can't do this." Lishia waited.

"Don't be too hasty. Let me talk to Dad. You know you have a birthday in January. We might be able to call part of this your present. And you could do some babysitting during the holidays. Remember last year when you babysat on New Year's Eve and made such good money?"

"Yes, but—"

"And Lishia, have you prayed about this?"

Lishia gave her a blank look.

"Because you know if this is God's will, he can provide for you, right?"

"Yes, but—"

"So that is just what we'll do. We'll pray about it. And while I'm at it, I'd like to pray about the girl too. What's her name?"

"Gillian Rodowski."

"Rodowski?" Mom tilted her head to one side. "That's not a common name."

"So?"

"Well, there's a Mrs. Rodowski at my school this year. I barely know her, but she recently took over a fifth-grade class during Mrs. Spencer's maternity leave. I remember hearing her saying something about a teenage daughter. Do you think that could be the same Rodowski?"

"I have absolutely no idea." Suddenly Lishia was uneasy. Hopefully Mom did not actually know Gillian's mother. "But I will say this—Gillian is not too happy that I'm replacing her. I think she might even hold me personally responsible for her downfall."

"But you said she got arrested for underage drinking. How could that be your fault?"

"I know." Lishia took a soda from the fridge. "But I think she wants to blame everyone and anyone."

"Just the same, I will be praying for her," Mom assured her. "And for you too. Our God is big enough to provide what you need for cheerleading." Her smile reappeared. "I'm so proud of you, sweetie!"

Lishia gave a stiff smile. "Thanks." But as she walked to

her room, she felt like a heel. Her shoes might be sevens, but she was a size thirteen heel. And she didn't want to think about what Mom had said about praying. Praying was the last thing on Lishia's mind these days. Even if she wanted to pray—and she didn't—she seriously doubted that God would want to listen.

nine

On Thanksgiving, Lishia's entire family was supportive and celebratory over her new role as a varsity cheerleader. So much so that she could almost make herself believe that it truly was a good thing—that she'd earned it.

"This is to help you with your rally girl outfit," Grandma Willis said as she tucked a fifty-dollar bill into Lishia's hand.

"Oh, Grandma—this is too—"

"Don't argue with your elders," Grandma warned as she pulled on her coat. "I want you to make us proud, Lishia. And I plan to come to some of your games. You know I used to be a rally girl too"—she chuckled—"back in the dark ages."

Before she left, Aunt Jamie gave Lishia a twenty. "I know it won't get you much," she admitted, "but maybe it'll help a little."

"See, God is already providing," Mom said when Lishia showed her the money.

"And I'll pay you another twenty," Dad told Lishia, "if you give your mom a break and clean the kitchen."

Mom started to protest, saying it was too much work for one person, but Lishia insisted it was a good idea and told Mom to go put her feet up. In a way, Lishia was glad to be by herself in the kitchen. It almost seemed like a form of penance—not that she believed in that sort of thing, but she still felt guilty for all the positive attention she was getting for making cheerleader. What would her family say if they knew the rest of the sordid story? As she scrubbed the greasy pots, she told herself that eventually it would all sift out and settle down and she'd feel like her normal self again. She just needed to be patient.

Over the next few days, Lishia practiced with the other cheerleaders, and by Monday she thought she was finally over the hump—she actually felt like she was one of them with as much right to be there as anyone.

"You're a fast learner," Amanda told her as they finished up practice on Monday afternoon.

"Thanks." Lishia smiled. "I guess you guys are all good teachers."

"Keep it up and you'll eventually be as good as Gillian," Vanessa said.

"She's already that good," Riley countered.

"I wouldn't go that far." Vanessa scowled at Riley.

"I wouldn't either," Lishia said quickly. "Gillian really was good. I still feel sad for her."

Riley rolled her eyes as she wiped her brow with a sweat towel.

"Gillian is having a real hard time with everything," Vanessa quietly confided to Lishia. "She called me this weekend and we talked for a couple of hours. She was crying most of the time."

"Poor Gillian." Amanda shook her head. "I guess it's a lesson for all of us."

They all acted like this was true, like they would never make the same mistakes that Gillian had made, and everyone promised to be nicer to Gillian.

"Like that's going to happen," Riley whispered to Lishia as they went into the locker room.

Lishia tossed her a warning look, but Riley just rolled her eyes again. At times like this Lishia wished that Riley wasn't her "best" friend. In fact, Lishia wished a lot of things that weren't likely to come true. For instance, it seemed that despite how she was beginning to fit in with these girls, it was still completely impossible that she could have a uniform in time for their first game—even if they put a rush on the order, like Mrs. Glassman had suggested today, it was unlikely it would arrive in time since the company said it would take two weeks minimum.

As she got dressed, Lishia started to wonder if all this practicing with the team wasn't a big waste of everyone's time—or maybe these hard workouts would be her punishment—because eventually she'd have to concede that she couldn't get that much money together, and they'd have to go with the second alternate.

"You're being awfully quiet," Riley said as she drove Lishia home.

"I guess I'm kinda bummed."

"You're not still riddled with guilt over poor little Gillian?" Riley sounded disgusted.

"No," Lishia snapped. "I just don't see how I can possibly

get enough money to order what I need in time for the first game."

"You mean you haven't ordered yet?"

"No, of course not. I don't have the money yet."

"Well, you better get on it, Lishia." She sounded seriously irritated. "I didn't work this hard to get you on the squad just to have you let us down."

"*You* worked hard?" Lishia frowned. "What about me?"

"Are you kidding? I worked a lot harder than you for this." Riley stopped at an intersection and turned to glare at Lishia. "I risked everything for you."

"How?"

"For starters, I broke into Glassman's computer, remember?"

Lishia nodded soberly. She had nearly forgotten that little part. "Even so, I didn't ask you to do that. And it didn't make any difference as far as me being part of the team."

"That's what you think."

"Huh?"

"What if I told you I'd tampered with the votes?"

"You tampered with the votes? Yeah, right!"

Riley pressed her lips tightly together—almost as if she hadn't meant to say that.

"You didn't really tamper with the votes, did you?"

"Never mind!" Riley lurched the car out into the intersection and let out a foul word.

"No, I want to know. What did you mean by that?"

Riley said nothing as she turned onto Lishia's street.

"Out with it," Lishia insisted. "Spill the beans, Riley. What did you do?"

"Fine." Riley parked in front of Lishia's house. "If you

must know, you were the second alternate—not the first. Are you happy now?"

"*Second?*" Lishia gasped. "I was second? Then why am I—"

"Because I fixed it, okay?"

"Fixed it?"

"Yes. I got into Glassman's computer and I simply re-arranged the numbers to make sure you'd get on."

"When did you do all this?"

"Right after you and I became friends." Riley looked hope-fully at Lishia. "I did it for you, Lish. I could tell we were going to be best friends, and I wanted you to be a cheerleader."

"So what you told me, early on, about how I was first alternate . . . that was all a great big lie?"

"Of course it was a lie. Michelle was first alternate, but she probably would've been disqualified for grades and stuff. You actually lost by quite a few votes. You should thank me." Riley glared at her. "Instead of acting like a totally spoiled brat."

"I should thank you?" Lishia was thinking that Riley had ruined her life—and for what? Seriously, who was the spoiled brat here? For several seconds the girls locked angry eyes and neither of them said a word. Lishia was too enraged to speak. How had she let herself get into this mess?

Suddenly Riley's scowl faded into a slightly catty smile. "Don't you start getting any heroic ideas about undoing this by ratting on me. Because I swear, if you tell anyone, we will both go down—big time. I will make it look like it was all your idea, and everyone will believe me. After all, you were the one with the most to gain here. I was already a cheerleader, remember? So don't kid yourself, Lishia—you are in this as thick as I am. No, thicker."

Lishia tightened her grip on her bag, suppressing the urge to scream and cry and throw a hissy fit. What was wrong with Riley? Oh, yeah, besides being spoiled and manipulative and used to getting her own way—other than that she was just great. Who could ask for a better friend?

"Look," Riley said in a gentle tone. "Just go with it, Lishia. Can't you see it's for the best . . . for everyone? Even if you tried to tell on me, you know I would deny it. And then I would tell what I know about you."

"What do you *know*?"

"Just that you went after Gillian first. You provoked her for no reason. Remember when you told her she stunk? There were other girls in the bathroom that night. Amanda would back me. So would Vanessa. We could make it look like you planned this whole thing—right from the get-go. And why not? You had everything to gain. And you know that Coach Glassman's sympathy is already with Gillian."

Lishia was too stunned to respond. Her so-called best friend was threatening blackmail.

"Don't be mad, Lishia. It's just the way it is." Riley patted her on the shoulder. "Like I said, in the end it's the best—for everyone. Even Gillian. I heard that Coach Glassman is encouraging her to get some counseling help and alcohol treatment."

"Right . . ." Lishia gritted her teeth as she reached for the door handle.

"You just need to cool off," Riley told her. "Then we need a plan for helping you to get that uniform. Call me tonight and let's brainstorm some kind of fundraiser idea. Okay?" She had switched over to her nice, sweet, little girl voice. "We're still friends, aren't we?"

Lishia shrugged. "See ya." She got out of the car, slammed the door, then took several deep breaths as she walked up to the house. She needed to get a grip on her anger before Mom asked her how her day went. She didn't want to explode and let all this out, didn't want Mom to know the truth. But she had to come up with a way out of this—and being without the funds to order her uniform and things seemed the perfect escape.

"Hello?" Mom called from the kitchen. "Is that you, Lishia?"

"Hey," Lishia answered. "I'm going to my room now."

"Not yet!" Mom called back urgently. "I have a surprise for you first!"

Lishia braced herself, trying to paste a happy expression on her face for whatever it was that Mom had, probably a cupcake left over from one of her students' birthday parties. "What is it?" Lishia asked glumly as she came in the kitchen.

"Ta-da!" Mom waved her arms to display a huge arrangement of white and purple items spread all over the kitchen countertops.

Lishia's eyes grew wide as she realized what she was looking at. *"What?"*

"Everything you need for cheerleading." Mom beamed proudly at her. "Can you believe it?"

"Huh?"

"They were Gillian's." Mom was actually dancing around the kitchen now. "Isn't it wonderful?"

Lishia spirits plummeted even deeper. "Gillian's?"

"Yes. I made a fantastic deal with her mom. She was actually glad to get rid of the stuff. She's so disappointed with Gillian."

"Gillian was willing to sell this stuff to me?" Lishia picked up a pom-pom and gave it a pathetic shake.

"Gillian didn't have a choice in the matter. Cindy Rodowski told me that her daughter only earned a small part of the money, and Cindy had to pay for the rest. At the time she didn't mind because she thought it was what Gillian needed, you know, to help her get her life on track. But then when it all unraveled, well, let's just say Cindy wasn't too happy. In fact, she said it was like a slap in the face, like Gillian didn't appreciate Cindy's sacrifices."

"Oh . . ." Lishia set the pom-pom back down and sighed.

"I thought you'd be thrilled." Mom smiled victoriously. "I know Cindy was hugely relieved to be rid of it—and even make some money. She actually ran home during lunch and loaded it all up in her car. They've been under a lot of financial pressure, and even though she only charged me a fraction of what this stuff is worth, she seemed genuinely happy to get the money. You can pay me back for part of it, and we'll call the rest your birthday present." Mom picked up a pom-pom and shook it. "Rah! Rah! Rah!"

"I, uh, I don't know what to say." Lishia really had no words—no words she wanted her mom to hear, anyway.

"How about, *Thanks, Mom—you're the greatest?*" Mom grinned. "Or maybe you can do a cheer for me."

"Thanks, Mom, you really are the greatest." Lishia forced a happy face. "Can you take a rain check on the cheer? I've got a bunch of homework."

"Sure." Mom gathered up an armload of stuff. "You get the rest of this and we'll pack it all to your room."

As Lishia gathered an armload of clothes, she smelled

something unpleasant. "Oh, that's right, I almost forgot something."

"Forgot what?"

"Gillian has really strong BO."

Mom chuckled, then took a sniff. "Oh . . . yeah, I see what you mean."

"Do you think we can wash it all first?"

"Sure. Let's drop the clothes in the laundry room. I'll get to it later." She held up a pair of shoes. "And do you know that Gillian's feet are only a half size larger than yours? I thought maybe an extra pair of socks and you'd be okay. Some of these shoes are barely worn, honey."

Lishia couldn't bear to imagine how Gillian must be feeling. She dumped the clothes into an empty laundry basket. "I sure hope that smell comes out," she said to Mom.

"I'll use some special detergent," Mom assured her. "We'll get rid of it."

"Thanks." Lishia gave her a genuine smile. "You're one in a million, Mom."

"Glad you appreciate me. And I know you won't let me down." She ran her hand over Lishia's head. "Not like Gillian did with her mom."

Lishia turned away so Mom couldn't see her eyes. Once again, she felt on the verge of frustrated tears. She felt like she was digging herself deeper and deeper into a hole—a big black hole with no way out.

※

For the rest of the week, Lishia played the part of the happy, perky cheerleader as well as the dutiful best friend, always saying and doing the right things—whatever it took to keep

Riley content. It was easier that way. Riley never seemed to guess Lishia was acting, and by Friday, thoroughly exhausted, Lishia was thankful the week was finally ending.

"I told Dayton that you and Todd would go to the movies with us tonight," Riley informed Lishia as she dropped her off.

"But I—"

"No buts, Lishia." Riley cut her off. "This is the last Friday for a while without a ball game. We need to make the most of it."

"Why didn't Todd ask me himself?"

"He had to get to basketball practice."

Lishia knew Todd was on varsity, so that was probably true. They were trying to get ready for next week's first game.

"Dayton said around seven, okay?"

"Okay . . ." Lishia got out of the car and faked a cheerful wave. "See ya!"

Riley zipped off, and Lishia stood there shaking her head. It was as if she had become Riley's slave friend. Lishia would probably never get to have her own opinions, make her own choices . . . it was an awfully high price to pay for a "best" friend. But there seemed no way out. As Lishia went in the house, she remembered how she used to complain about Janelle sometimes. Janelle had been stubborn and even a pain at times, but she was an angel compared to Riley. Being best friends with Riley was a nightmare. A never-ending nightmare.

ten

"You seem different," Todd told Lishia as he walked her to the door after their double date with Riley and Dayton.

"How so?" she asked absently.

"I don't know." He frowned. "But you're not the same fun-loving girl you used to be." He grinned. "Remember my birthday party and how we ran from the cops?"

"Shhh . . ." She put a finger over her lips. "I don't want my parents hearing that."

"See." He nodded. "You are different."

"Maybe I'm just tired."

He shrugged. "Yeah . . . maybe."

"Thanks for the movie and everything," she told him as she reached for the doorknob.

"Sure." He stepped back and shook his head like he was disappointed.

"I'm sorry you think I'm different," she told him.

"Hey, you can't help what you are." He gave a plastic-looking smile. "See ya around, Lish." Then he turned and jogged back to the car. As she watched him go, she knew it was over. Her chance to be Todd's girl had just blown up in her face. She knew it was her own stupid fault, but the truth was, she didn't really care. It was as if it was all too much.

Trying to keep up the cheerleader happy face, trying to play Riley's loyal best friend . . . it was all sucking the life out of her. She had no energy left to play Todd's fun-loving girlfriend. And although part of her felt like crying, the larger part of her felt numb . . . and dead. She knew she had disconnected herself from God and that there was no point in taking her troubles to him. As a result, she felt more alone than ever.

⁂

"What happened between you and Todd?" Riley demanded on the phone the next day.

"Nothing."

"But he said you guys broke up."

"Then I guess we did." Lishia flopped down on her bed and sighed.

"Why?"

"I don't know why . . . it just wasn't working."

"But Todd's a great guy—and he and Dayton are such good friends. I had plans for us to go to prom together and—"

"Prom? That's, like, months away, Riley. I can't even wrap my head around next week."

"Speaking of next week, Amanda called and wants to have a practice at her house. She says we need to work on that halftime routine and I agree. I'll pick you up at four thirty, okay?"

"Okay."

"Is something wrong?"

"No." Lishia tried to perk up her voice. "I was just sleepy."

"See you at four thirty."

Lishia agreed and closed her phone. She had really hoped to go to youth group tonight—she knew she needed it, maybe more than ever. But if practice lasted the usual couple of hours, she would be cutting it pretty close. Still, maybe it was possible. Lishia opened her phone and punched Megan Bernard's number. Megan had been nagging Lishia all week—okay, maybe *nagging* was the wrong word—Megan had been *encouraging* Lishia to return to youth group. And yesterday Lishia had promised to try.

"Hey, Megan," she said cheerfully. "You still want to give me a ride to youth group tonight?"

"Sure." Megan sounded a little skeptical. "You really want to come?"

"I do. But I have cheerleading practice at Amanda's house. Would you mind picking me up there?"

"This isn't a trick, is it?"

"No, of course not. Practice will probably end around seven. I know that will make us a few minutes late. Do you mind?"

"No, that's okay."

Lishia told her the address. "And I'd really like to talk to you, Megan."

"To me?"

"Well, I need to talk to someone . . . someone who's a Christian, you know?"

"You can talk to me," Megan said.

"It's just that I'm feeling, well, kinda trapped."

"Trapped? How?"

"It's this whole cheerleader thing. I guess I kinda feel like

I got on this crazy roller-coaster ride and I don't know how to get off."

"You want to quit being a cheerleader?" Megan sounded shocked.

"I don't know . . . I'm not even sure. I guess I wonder how I can possibly be a cheerleader *and* a Christian. You know?"

"I guess I get that. But we are supposed to be lights in dark places. Maybe that's what you're doing. Besides, Amanda Jorgenson always claims to be a Christian, so it's not like you're alone."

"I know, but it's still hard. And being Riley's friend isn't easy either." Lishia knew she was saying a lot . . . maybe too much.

"Well, Riley has always been kind of manipulative, if you know what I mean."

"I guess . . ." Lishia stopped herself from saying how she really felt.

"I can understand how it might be hard being a Christian while you were Riley's best friend. I mean, that girl could probably influence you in some pretty bad directions, especially if you weren't careful." Megan paused. "But I don't want you to accuse me of gossiping again. I actually took what you said to heart. There's a fine line between repeating gossip and stating the truth. Several of us girls had a long talk with Raymond about this." Raymond was their youth pastor, and Lishia had always respected his opinions.

"What did he say?"

"He said one way to figure out if something is gossip or not was to ask yourself, 'Would I say this if the person I'm talking about was listening?'"

"That's good advice."

"So here is what I'd say if Riley was—" She stopped suddenly. "She's not listening, is she?"

"No, of course not."

"Okay, I'll have to trust you. I'd say Riley is probably a nice person, but she sometimes gives me the impression that she's using people to get what she wants. I could be wrong, but I've known Riley since middle school, and she hurt me a few times then and a few times since. I've learned to keep my distance from girls like that."

"Oh . . ."

"You have good friends in youth group," Megan told her. "Janelle and—"

"Janelle dumped me, remember?"

"Janelle said she didn't dump you. She said you got hurt because she wanted to include Chelsea as a friend and—"

"Janelle and Chelsea are best friends now. Or haven't you noticed?"

"Well, I guess that's true. But it's only because you stepped out of the picture. And Chelsea is really nice. If you got to know her, I'm sure you'd like her."

"What makes you so sure?" Lishia was feeling aggravated now.

"Well, if you can get along with someone like Riley, I should think Chelsea would be pretty refreshing. She's a strong Christian, and she's honest and kind and—"

"You know, I didn't call you to hear you singing Chelsea's praises, Megan. But thanks for—"

"Sorry, I'm just saying you have good friends at youth group. There's me and Grayson and Chase and—"

"Thanks, Megan. I know you're trying to help me, but

maybe this is all a bad idea." Lishia was pacing back and forth in her bedroom now.

"What's a bad idea?" Megan sounded hurt.

"Me coming to youth group with you. Maybe I'm really not ready for that." The truth was, Lishia was getting scared. She knew these kids well enough to know that they would see through her. They might even do something like offer to pray for her, and she could end up breaking down in tears and spilling the whole story. Then everyone would know!

"What did I say?" Megan asked helplessly. "I'm sorry if I stepped on your toes. You know me and my big mouth. Please, come to youth group with me, Lishia. You won't be sorry."

"I don't think it's a good idea. I mean, I do have practice, and sometimes we run late. I might end up making you so late that it wouldn't even be worth going. No, tonight's not a good night. Thanks, Megan. Maybe I can make it next week."

"But Lishia!"

"No, I've made up my mind. I can't do it tonight. But I'll think about it for next week. Thanks, Megan. Later!" Lishia hung up and flopped back onto her bed. That was close! What had she been thinking? Of course, she couldn't show up at youth group and expect that her friends could help her without her spilling all the beans in front of them. Seriously, had she lost her ever-loving mind?

❧

Lishia felt like she was going to throw up on Friday afternoon. To kick off basketball season, the school had a big pep assembly. It would be her first time performing as a varsity cheerleader, and she knew she was going to either fall on her face or fall completely apart.

"I can't do this," she muttered from the bathroom stall where she was holed up.

"Yes, you can," Riley hissed at her. "And you will!"

"Come on," Vanessa urged. "It's almost time to start."

"I can't," Lishia sobbed. "I'm sick."

"You are not sick," Riley snapped. "You're just a chicken."

"I'm going out there now," Vanessa said angrily. "I'll see if I can get Amanda to stall a couple minutes, but if you're not there in five minutes, we're going on without you, Lishia. So get it together!"

"Come on," Riley commanded. "You're going to do this, Lishia, even if I have to drag you out myself."

"I can't."

"Stop being such a baby and come on!"

Lishia tore off a long strip of toilet paper and loudly blew her nose. "I wish I were dead," she mumbled.

"That could be arranged."

"Thanks."

"Look, Lishia, it's just the jitters," Riley's voice turned patient. "Everyone gets them. You have to ignore them. You've done really great in practice. Everyone says you're really good. And your jumps have gotten really spectacular. I've actually been a little jealous."

"Really?" Lishia sniffed.

"Yes, so come on. Let's just do this. You'll get it over with and you'll never feel like this again. I promise."

Lishia unlocked the door, and Riley jerked it open. "Now, come on!" She grabbed Lishia's arm and dragged her out. "Let's run."

Just as they entered the gym, the other cheerleaders from both varsity and JV ran out onto the floor with pom-poms in hand, getting into formation for the opening fight song routine that they were all supposed to perform together. Lishia and Riley ran out with them, and following everyone's lead, Lishia pasted a confident smile onto her face and took her place, and suddenly the jazz band was blasting out the fight song.

Focus, Lishia told herself as she counted the beats in her head and started in with the initial moves. She knew she wasn't giving a spectacular performance, but at least she was keeping time—and remembering the routine. A rush of relief swept over her as the song ended and they all did some jumps, trying to generate spirit and enthusiasm from the crowd.

The dance team came to the floor, preparing to do a routine while the JV cheerleaders got ready to do their skit. After the dance routine, the varsity cheerleaders took the floor again. This time Lishia felt a little more confident, but barely into the routine, she hit a slick spot on the gym floor and slipped, landing smack on her bottom, which sent the crowd into laughter. Naturally, the rest of the squad continued without her. She quickly got to her feet and, with a reddening face, attempted to get back into the yell, but she never quite made it.

"Way to go, Vance," someone in the stands yelled out as they finished. Lishia wanted to run, but she knew that wasn't going to work.

"Shake it off," Riley hissed in her ear. "Just smile. Act like you don't care and they won't care either."

During the JV skit, Lishia tried to get her head together, but all she could think was that this was all wrong—so wrong! What had ever made her think she wanted this—or had she even? She couldn't even remember. But now it was time to do another dance routine as the varsity basketball team came out to do some drills and get the crowd going.

Lishia tried to look happy, but she felt like a woodenheaded puppet as she went through the paces. Did anyone else know how ridiculous she felt? How silly all these moves and routines were . . . as if their gyrations could actually help the basketball team this year. Everyone knew they were ranked at the bottom of their league.

Mostly Lishia was thinking how glad she'd be when this assembly was over and she could go home. Of course, there'd still be the basketball game tonight—that would go on for hours . . . and the hours would feel like days . . . and what had she gotten herself into? And for what? As they ended the cheer, she glanced at Riley, who was jumping and grinning—thoroughly enjoying herself—and Lishia realized that her "best friend" was actually her puppeteer. Riley was the one pulling the strings to make Lishia jump. This image made her want to hurl for real.

eleven

Lishia heard the bathroom door open and close as she hid out in the stall, but she lifted her feet up so that whoever had come to this out-of-the-way restroom wouldn't see her shoes and guess who it was while she waited for them to do their business and leave.

At least the pep assembly was over now. Lishia wanted to lie low until the crowd thinned so she could gracefully (ha!) exit the athletic complex and call her mom for a ride. If Mom was busy, which was likely, she'd walk home. Or maybe she'd even ride the activities bus. It couldn't be any more humiliating than what she'd just experienced, plus she could avoid another dose of Riley's criticism.

Yes, Lishia knew she'd blown it out there. Not just when she fell on her backside—as if that wasn't bad enough! But she'd also completely blanked out on not one but two routines. Routines that she knew backward and forward and had been practicing for weeks. There was no good excuse for messing up like that. Now if whoever was in here would just leave!

"So was it worth it?"

A shock wave ran through Lishia—that voice sounded exactly like Gillian's.

"I know you're in there, Lishia."

"Gillian?" Lishia said in a shaky voice.

"Who are you hiding from, anyway?"

Lishia didn't know what to do. She hadn't actually had a conversation with Gillian since that unfortunate night at the birthday party—something she had been trying to forget.

"Come out, Lishia. I'm not going to hurt you . . . well, not too much anyway." Gillian gave a wicked laugh.

Lishia took a deep breath and considered the possibilities. There might be worse things than getting beat up by Gillian . . . like when she'd made a complete fool of herself at the assembly. And if Gillian beat her up badly enough, Lishia wouldn't have to go to the game tonight—she would have a perfectly good excuse.

"What do you want?" Lishia asked meekly as she slunk out of the stall, bracing herself for whatever was in store for her. Really, how bad could it be?

"Just to see you." Gillian scowled. "And to laugh in your face." She made an attempt at laughter. "By the way, you were pathetic out there! Seriously sad and an embarrassment to good cheerleaders everywhere."

"You don't think I know that?" Lishia returned her glare.

"So tell me, was it worth it?"

"Worth what?"

"All the work you went to, you know, to get me kicked off the squad."

"You got yourself kicked off."

"You're saying you had nothing to do with it?"

Lishia shrugged and walked over to the sinks, making a pretense of washing her hands extra thoroughly.

"You expect me to believe it was just a coincidence that you were right there, pestering me, waiting in the wings for me to blow it so bad that you could jump in and replace me?" Her voice was getting louder, and Lishia was getting nervous as she dried her hands. "Pretty convenient that our moms work at the same school—and how you literally stole my stuff from me." She grabbed the shoulder of Lishia's top, the top that used to be Gillian's and still smelled of her, and then she tugged it so hard that Lishia heard threads pop, and the two girls were eye to eye.

"I never asked my mom to do that," Lishia told her. "Believe me, I was as blindsided by that as you were."

"Yeah, right!" Gillian let her go so quickly that Lishia fell backward, hitting her elbow on the sink. And now she was mad—not just at Gillian, but at everyone! "You can be mad at me if you want!" she yelled straight into Gillian's face. "And maybe I even deserve some of it—but it's your own stupid fault you got kicked off. You were totally drunk at Todd's party—you made a complete fool of yourself! You know the code of conduct and you blew—"

"I was *not* totally drunk!" Gillian shrieked back at her.

"You were wasted," Lishia shot back. "Riley even taped you—and you didn't even know that, did you?"

"I had one drink!" Gillian held a finger in the air. "One stupid drink! And you can bet that Riley and Vanessa had at least that much."

"Right, you had one drink!" Lishia rolled her eyes. "Then I have to say, you really cannot hold your alcohol, Gillian. You really shouldn't drink at all if one single drink makes you act like an insane person. Seriously, what do you take me for, anyway?"

"I swear, I had one drink," Gillian seethed. Her face was just inches from Lishia's now, and her hand was balled into a tight fist, as if she was going to smack Lishia right in the face. "Someone was messing with—" She stopped as the bathroom door opened.

"Hey!" yelled Riley as she burst into the bathroom. "Back off, Gillian!"

Gillian's eyes grew wide as she dropped her fist to her side.

"Get in here, you guys," Riley screamed. "Gillian is beating up Lishia!"

Just like that, the other cheerleaders stormed the bathroom and surrounded Gillian, forming a barricade between her and Lishia. "Leave her alone," Krista, the biggest of the cheerleaders, yelled at Gillian as she simultaneously twisted Gillian's arm behind her back.

"Get her out of here," Amanda commanded. "Now!"

Vanessa and Krista escorted Gillian out.

"Are you okay?" Riley asked Lishia with what seemed to be real concern.

She nodded, standing up straight. "I'm fine."

"Did she hit you?" Amanda asked.

"No . . . but I think she was about to." Lishia sighed. "Thanks, you guys."

"What should we do with her?" Krista called from outside the bathroom.

Amanda looked curiously at Lishia.

"Just let her go," Lishia told her. "She didn't really do anything . . . I mean, besides yelling at me and acting tough. Besides . . . you can't really blame her for losing it."

"She looked like she was going to kill you," Riley insisted.

"But she didn't." Lishia gave a weak smile. "Maybe she just needed to vent a little. You know she's been through a lot these past few weeks."

Amanda put an arm around Lishia's shoulders. "It's sweet that you can see it that way, Lishia. You know, I'm liking you more and more." She squeezed her. "I know you messed up out there and you probably feel like giving up right now. But let's just consider that your initiation. Seriously, it can't get worse, can it? Now you need to relax and go with the flow. Stop taking it so seriously. We're just cheerleaders, for Pete's sake, not brain surgeons." She threw back her head and laughed. "Trust me, someday you'll look back on this and see how silly it all was."

Lishia thought she could see that right now. But Amanda's words were comforting. And it was kind of sweet how the cheerleaders showed up at just the right moment to rescue her. She guessed she owed them now. Besides, it wasn't their fault (except for Riley) that Lishia felt like she was in such a mess. For their sakes, she would have to try harder. She was determined to try harder.

"Lucky for you that Dayton saw you ducking into that restroom after the assembly," Riley told Lishia as she drove her home. "He was on his way to his locker when he saw Gillian head in there after you, and he got worried. He's the one who called to give me the heads up." Riley frowned. "But what I can't figure is why you took off like that and why on earth you went clear down there to use the restroom."

"There was a line at the other restroom," Lishia lied. "And I really needed to go—remember how my stomach was so upset? Well, I couldn't wait."

"Eww. Too much information." Riley turned up her nose. "Anyway, you owe Dayton one for being on it like he was."

"I'll try to remember to thank him."

"So are you going to be okay tonight?"

"Yeah." Lishia was determined to get a handle on this. "I'll keep what Amanda said in mind. I've already paid my dues. Time to move on."

Riley laughed. "Yeah, we've all had our embarrassing moments."

"Even you?"

Riley gave her a cool look. "Not really. I try to avoid those kinds of mishaps. But I do enjoy watching when others make fools of themselves. Unless it happens to be my best friend. Seriously, I don't need that."

For some reason Lishia was thinking about how Amanda and Riley used to be best friends—at least she thought they had been. Maybe she'd been wrong about that too. "I'm curious," she began cautiously. "Didn't you and Amanda used to be best friends?"

Riley shrugged.

"But then Gillian came between you, right?" Lishia studied Riley closely, trying to figure this out.

"Well, I'll admit it was pretty irritating when Amanda started taking Gillian's side over mine, but I suppose Amanda and I weren't really best, best friends." She smiled. "Not like you and I are."

"Oh . . ."

"I don't think Amanda actually has a best friend. She's not like that."

Now that Riley said this, Lishia thought perhaps it was true. She had never seen Amanda really paired up with one particular girl—not for long, anyway. It was more like Amanda was *everyone's* friend. Not an easy act necessarily. Not that Lishia thought it was an act . . . but it was sort of odd. Yet it was admirable too, in a way, although Lishia wasn't sure she'd ever be able to pull it off.

"I'll pick you up at five thirty," Riley said as Lishia was getting out.

"Five thirty?" Lishia frowned. "Why so early?"

"You know we have to attend the JV games."

"We do?"

"It's part of the cheerleaders' contract. Didn't you even read it?"

"Yes . . ." Lishia nodded. "Guess I forgot that part."

"Well, after your performance today you can't exactly afford to start blowing the contract." She laughed. "You might end up like Gillian."

Lishia forced a smile, but she was thinking there were worse things. At least Gillian was free now. Although, come to think of it, Gillian didn't seem any too happy about it.

As Lishia went into the house, she wondered if everyone wasn't in some kind of trap—stuck doing something they really didn't want to do, but with no way out. Maybe it was just how life was supposed to be. Maybe she should simply get used to it.

With that in mind, Lishia decided that she needed to bite the bullet and go for it at the game tonight. She'd been pretending about most everything anyway, at least during these past few weeks, so maybe all this was simply preparing her to become an actress. Maybe she would switch from art to drama next term—except that she really liked art!

Shortly before the JV game ended, Lishia decided to make

Amanda her new role model. She would pattern herself after her. The way Amanda encouraged the other cheerleaders, both JV and varsity, the way she kept a positive attitude, the way she could put a happy spin on anything . . . well, it was inspiring to say the least. Amanda was the quintessential perfect cheerleader, and if Lishia could be a little bit like her, it would be a huge improvement.

Ironically, it seemed to help Lishia when it came to being in front of the crowd too. She made fewer mistakes and was less concerned about it when she did. She knew her parents and Grandma Willis were in the stands tonight too. But to her relief, she wasn't obsessing over this. She was simply in the moment—and to her surprise, it was fun. Maybe this was how Amanda felt too.

It wasn't until the end of the varsity game, which they lost, that Lishia began to get a clue as to why Amanda was like this. Lishia wasn't even sure if she was right or not, but it was her new theory, and she planned to cling to it.

The reason Amanda was such a great cheerleader was because she didn't focus on herself. Not the way others did, anyway. The other cheerleaders, especially Riley, seemed all-consumed with their images, like whether or not their lip gloss was shining, their hair was looking perfect, their jumps were the highest, their position in the lineup was the best, and so on and so forth. It was all about them. Not so with Amanda.

The unusual thing about Amanda, and probably the reason she made such a good captain, was that she seemed concerned with the group as a whole. She put her energy into making the others both look and feel good. There was no doubt that she wanted everyone to be at their best—but she wanted them to be at their best together, as a team. It was rather refreshing. And it gave Lishia hope.

After the game, everyone went to Allegro's as usual. But tonight Lishia made an effort to stay close to Amanda, even sitting next to her. This wasn't easy since it seemed everyone wanted to be her friend. But to continue her observations, Lishia felt it was imperative to have a front-row seat. Throughout the evening, Amanda continued treating others as if she genuinely liked them, as if they were truly special. She seemed unconcerned over the fact that her hair was a little messy or that her lip gloss had worn thin. She was simply in the moment, being kind and funny and real. And Lishia couldn't help but admire her even more.

"What is it with you?" Riley asked as they were leaving. "It's like you're obsessed with Amanda now."

"So sue me. But I think she's really nice," Lishia admitted. "I was curious how she does it."

"She might be nice, but she's boring as it gets."

"I don't agree."

"Maybe it's because you're boring too." Riley laughed.

"Thanks a lot."

"Sorry. But I need a best friend who's fun, Lishia, and I'm starting to get seriously concerned about you."

"So you don't think Amanda is fun?"

"No." She said this like it should be obvious. "Do you?"

"I don't know her well enough to really say. But I do admire her. She seems, well, I can't think of the word . . . maybe *authentic*."

"Authentic?" Riley laughed really hard now. "You've got to be kidding. Amanda is a fake."

"A fake?"

"Yeah, she acts like she's everyone's best friend. How unreal is that?"

"Maybe she's naturally nice."

"That's ridiculous."

"You're just jaded, Riley. You think everyone is like you."

"Excuse me for being a realist. I can see right through Amanda. She's a big fake."

"You're wrong. Amanda is the real deal." Lishia nodded her head. "She's authentic. I'm sure of it."

"If Amanda's authentic, I'm a saint."

"Well, you're definitely not a saint." Lishia pressed her lips together, controlling herself from saying what she really thought about Riley and sainthood.

"I can't believe you would fall for her little act, Lishia. Seriously, Amanda is the biggest phony of all."

"Why do you say that?" Lishia felt indignant.

"Because she pretends to like everyone. No one can possibly like *everyone*."

"Why would she pretend? What would be the point?"

"Because her life is a perennial popularity contest."

"A what?" Lishia blinked.

"A perennial popularity contest. She's like that girl on *The Bachelor*, the one who befriends every single girl there and just wants to be liked, or else she's the beauty contestant who wants to win Miss Congeniality. But do you know what those girls get for their hard work?"

"What?"

"Nothing. They lose the bachelor . . . and lose the beauty pageant. Those goody-two-shoes end up with nothing but a bunch of phony-baloney friends who don't honestly care whether they live or die."

"That's pretty harsh."

"That's life. Like I said, I'm a realist."

Lishia wanted to tell Riley that she was seriously twisted, but she didn't want to start a big fight, especially when she was nearly home and looking forward to escaping her BFF—beast friend forever! "Thanks for the ride." She forced some sweetness into her voice. "Tonight was fun!"

"Ugh, now you're even starting to sound like Amanda."

"Sorry." Lishia smiled, thinking that maybe this would be a way to lose this binding relationship with Riley. Act like Amanda, and Riley would probably drop her like a bad case of acne.

"There's a party at Vanessa's tomorrow," Riley told her. "I want you to go with me."

"Why don't you go with Dayton?" Lishia suggested.

"Because I want to go with you."

"But aren't you and Dayton going out—"

"I don't want Dayton to start thinking he owns me again, Lishia. Don't you get it? The way you keep a guy is to keep him guessing." She shook her head like Lishia was a complete idiot. "You have so much to learn."

"Clearly." Lishia waved politely and closed the door. But as she walked to the house, she imagined all that she would like to say to Riley. Not that Riley was ever likely to listen.

twelve

As irritating as Riley could be, she could also turn on the charm when she wanted to. Maybe she was sorry for being so rude recently, or maybe she was just trying to get her way, but Lishia could tell Riley was trying to be nice when she called on Saturday afternoon.

"Please, come with me," Riley begged. "Macy's is having a huge sale, and you're so much fun to shop with. And you have such good taste."

Lishia had to laugh at that. "Well, even if I actually had good taste, the problem is, I'm broke."

"That doesn't matter. You can still help me shop, can't you? And I'll treat you to lunch. Come on, it'll be fun. Remember the time we went shopping and got your hair done—and how much fun we had that day?"

Lishia wasn't sure if Riley wanted to remind her of the "fun" they'd had or of the fact that she still owed Riley for the blonde in her hair—another form of Riley's blackmail. "Okay," she reluctantly agreed, "I'll go with you."

"Yay! I'll pick you up in a few minutes."

Lishia had mixed feelings as she got ready to go. On one hand, Riley could be fun sometimes, and she could be pretty generous . . . on the other hand, she could also be a royal pain. And more and more, Lishia felt she had absolutely no control over this relationship. It was like Riley had all the power and Lishia had no choice but to comply with her demands. Riley could say, "Jump," and Lishia would ask, "How high?"

But since there seemed to be no way out of this twisted friendship, at least for now, perhaps the best thing to do was to try to keep Riley happy, even if it did make Lishia feel like a complete hypocrite. Maybe in time, Riley would get tired of her—especially if Lishia continued imitating Amanda.

"Where are you off to?" Dad asked as Lishia emerged from her room.

"Riley wants me to go shopping." She shrugged. "But I don't have to—I mean if there's something you—"

"No, no, you should go and have some fun," he told her. "You've worked so hard these past few weeks, learning all your cheerleading routines and stuff. You probably need a break."

She nodded.

"Your mom just went for groceries, and I plan to turn on football and transform myself into a couch potato." He grinned. "Hey, we were so proud of you last night, Lish. Your grandma went on and on about how you girls were so talented. And we were so impressed with how well you kept up with the team. No one would've guessed that you were the newcomer."

"Thanks, Dad."

He reached in his back pocket. "And if you're going shopping, don't you need a little cash?" He winked. "Just don't tell your mom. She'll think I'm soft." He handed her a twenty. "You probably can't get much with that, but at least they can't pick you up for vagrancy."

She smiled as she tucked the bill into her purse. "Thanks, Dad." She knew their budget was tight—and paying for all her cheerleading stuff, although a bargain, had not been cheap.

Lishia had never been big into shopping. This was partially due to money—or a lack of it. But besides that, she thought it always seemed boring after a while. Really, how many pairs of jeans did one girl need? However, Riley seemed to think of shopping as a competitive sport—and she loved keeping up with the new trends. By the time Riley was ready to go, Lishia was exhausted.

"I really don't want to go to Vanessa's party," she told Riley as they walked out to the car.

"You have to go!" Riley insisted.

"Why?"

"Because I refuse to go alone."

"Go with Dayton."

"I already told Dayton I was going with you and that I'd see him there. I can't change that now." She popped open her trunk and tossed her bags in. "Don't be so flaky, Lishia."

"What kind of party is it, anyway?" Lishia scowled as she got in the car. Like she didn't know what kind of party it was!

"It's a Christmas party."

"Right, a Christmas party." Lishia sighed. "So everyone will be celebrating the birth of Christ then?"

Riley laughed.

"I really should go to youth group tonight. In fact, I should make you go with me. We need some good influence in our lives."

Now Riley laughed harder. "You are really cracking me up, Lishia."

"I'm serious. I feel like I'm losing my faith."

"Maybe you never had it to begin with."

Lishia considered this. Maybe Riley was right. Whatever the case, Lishia felt like a really bad example of a Christian. She hadn't prayed or read her Bible in weeks. Her Christian friends never even talked to her anymore, except for Megan, who made occasional attempts to preach at her, warning her that she was going the wrong direction. Maybe Lishia really had lost her faith. Because really, how could she expect that God would want anything to do with her anymore? When she thought of all the things she'd compromised in herself . . . just to be Riley's friend . . . it made her feel sick inside.

"Back to the party," Riley said. "I might want you to drive my car home. So why don't you spend the night at my house, okay?"

"So does that mean you'll be drinking?" Lishia felt a rush of anger.

"No, it means I might leave with Dayton. Or I might not."

"Oh . . ." Lishia wished there was an easy way to get out of going tonight. But maybe Riley would leave early with Dayton and Lishia would be free to go too. And maybe it really was a Christmas party. "Do you think Amanda will be there tonight?" she asked hopefully.

"Are you still nurturing your girl-crush on stupid Amanda?"

"It's not a girl-crush and she's not stupid."

"Well, I have no idea if Miss Perfect will be there or not. Do you want to call her and see if she'll make a date with you?"

"Funny." Lishia folded her arms in front of her and glared out the window. Why did Riley have to be so mean? And why did Riley feel the need to act like she owned Lishia's soul? Maybe it was because Lishia had sold it to her.

"We have to dress up," Riley said as they got out of the car.

"Why?"

"Because Vanessa said it was a Christmas party and she wants us to be festive and to dress up, but you can wear something of mine."

"Why didn't Vanessa invite me to her Christmas party herself?"

"You mean you didn't get the engraved invitation with the RSVP?" Riley teased.

"No, as a matter of fact, I didn't."

"These parties are always word-of-mouth, Lishia. Did you really not know that?" She handed one of her shopping bags to Lishia with a disappointed expression.

Lishia shrugged. "Anyway, I still need to call my mom. I told her I was going to the party, but I didn't know I was going to spend the night here. She might not want me to . . ." Okay, Lishia knew that was lame. Her mom would probably be glad to have her spend the night. She'd even complained about how Lishia had been spending too much time at home this fall, after her friendship with Janelle had disintegrated. In fact, Mom was delighted with Lishia's new "best friend"—much happier than Lishia was!

They spent a couple hours dressing and primping, and Lishia tried to convince herself that Vanessa's Christmas party might actually be fun. And maybe Amanda would be there. "So you don't think this party is going to be busted?" Lishia asked as they walked up to Vanessa's house, which was lit up with colorful Christmas lights. "Because I don't think I can run very fast in these heels."

"You better not run in those shoes," Riley warned her. "They're Marc Jacobs, the real deal."

"And a little big too," Lishia said as her heel slipped again. "I hope I don't trip and fall on my face." She looked at the expensive cars lining the long driveway. "These don't look like high school kids' cars," she said as they went to the front door.

"That's because it's Vanessa's parents' Christmas party," Riley told her impatiently. "I thought you knew that."

"No, I didn't know that. Why are we going to her parents' party?" Lishia stopped walking. "Isn't that a little weird?"

"No, Vanessa's parents are cool. They always let Vanessa invite her friends to their parties. It's their way of showing her off. The kids usually end up in the basement and the grown-ups stay upstairs, but the food is always good."

Lishia felt slightly relieved now. Having Vanessa's parents around should calm things down a lot. Maybe this would actually be fun—certainly the police wouldn't be involved tonight.

However, Lishia was barely inside the house when she realized that Vanessa's parents were a lot different than Lishia's. For one thing, they seemed a lot younger than parents should be, but maybe that was because this was Vanessa's mom's second marriage and Vanessa's new stepdad was only ten years older than Vanessa—and both of them were dressed like teenagers! But that wasn't the worst of it—the really disturbing thing was that Vanessa's parents had no problem with underage drinking.

"All the kids in Europe drink with their families," Vanessa's mom was telling a woman. "It teaches them to drink moderately."

The woman nodded. "Yes, I'd rather my kids learn to be responsible now than after they go away to college."

A jazz trio was playing in a corner of the great room, several couples were dancing, and it seemed the party was in full swing. But all Lishia could think was that she wanted to go home! Of course, Amanda was not there. She knew better than to get mixed up with something like this.

Lishia thought about the cheerleaders' conduct code and how many cheerleaders were breaking it tonight. What was the point of the code if no one, besides Amanda and Lishia, took it seriously? What would Mrs. Glassman say if she could see her girls now? Oh, sure, everyone was dressed nicely and using their "grown-up" manners, and instead of drinking from red plastic cups, they were sipping from sparkling glass-ware. Riley was being handed something in a martini glass, and she sipped it like she thought she was all that.

Lishia considered calling her parents, but then she'd have to explain all this. And what if Dad decided it was his parental responsibility to report the underage drinking? How would she ever live that down? No, she decided, she'd gotten herself into this situation, and she would need to get herself out of it.

Fortunately, Dayton showed up, and he and Riley paired up and even danced a few times. It seemed everyone—everyone but Lishia—was having a great time.

"Do you mind if I drive your car home now?" Lishia asked Riley after they'd been there for about an hour and the party was getting louder and crazier.

"No, you can't leave yet," Riley told her. "My parents will still be up, and they'll want to know why I'm not with you."

Lishia frowned. "So I'm stuck here?"

"Have a drink," Dayton told her. "Relax a little."

"I don't want to relax," Lishia told him. "I want to go home."

"Don't be such a party pooper," Riley told her. Then she grabbed Dayton's hand. "Let's go dance again."

Lishia watched as they went over to where Todd and Vanessa were already dancing. Despite herself, Lishia felt a stab of envy at seeing those two together. She knew she'd had her chance with Todd and she'd blown it. All because she didn't want to drink and be a party girl. He'd told her she was no fun. And here she was again—having no fun! It didn't seem fair.

She wandered into a quieter room. A small group of grown-ups was enjoying a lively political debate on one end of the room; meanwhile, a couple was snuggled into a love seat, whispering and giggling with their heads close together.

Taking a seat on a chair next to the tall Christmas tree by the window, she stared at the colorful lights and sighed. Her life used to be a lot more fun than this. She used to love Christmastime. She used to love lots of things—including God. Now it seemed like she didn't love anything—or anyone—not even herself. She felt empty and slightly dead inside. Everyone else in this house seemed to be having the time of their lives. And here she was feeling alone and depressed. What was wrong with her?

Oh, she knew what was wrong . . . she just didn't want to admit it. Not to herself, not to anyone. She'd managed to repress it all this time, and she'd probably have to repress it for the rest of her life. But the truth was, she had shoved God right out of her life, and now it felt like it was too late. She'd stepped over that line and there was no turning back. She felt hopeless and sad.

For the first time in her life, she thought she might understand why some people drank alcohol. It was probably to escape from something like this. And right now, more than ever, she wanted to escape too. So, she reasoned, perhaps one little drink wouldn't hurt. No one else seemed worried.

And maybe Vanessa's mom was right. Maybe it was time for Lishia to learn to drink responsibly, moderately, appropriately. Yes, she decided as she stood, it was high time for her to grow up!

thirteen

As Lishia made her way toward the bar, she spotted Todd and several others gathered over by the dancing area. They all had drinks in their hands and were smiling and laughing, acting like they were having a fabulous time, looking like a magazine advertisement for some kind of alcoholic beverage. Lishia imagined herself walking up to the group with a drink in her hand. She would casually greet them—act as if she were one of them. Todd would be surprised that she was drinking . . . then his eyes would light up as he saw her in a whole new light. Soon they would be dancing and—

"Someone as gorgeous as you shouldn't be alone, Lishia Vance."

She turned to see Brandon Procter smiling hopefully at her. She didn't know Brandon too well, but Riley liked him. It seemed they were always sharing some private joke, and Lishia suspected he had a secret crush on Riley, but she was a little out of his league. "Does that line usually work for you?" she said teasingly.

"Oh, you cut me to the core." He put his hand to his chest like her words had hurt. "But seriously, you do look gorgeous tonight." His smile reappeared.

"Thanks, Brandon, you're sweet."

"I don't want to be sweet." He took a sip of his drink and scowled.

"Sorry." She shrugged, glancing back to where Todd was now dancing with Vanessa again. Maybe she was too late.

"There are two things wrong with you tonight," Brandon held up two fingers and grimly shook his head.

She frowned at him. "What?"

"First of all, you're alone."

"Oh . . ."

"And that seems wrong."

She nodded. "I agree. What's the other thing?"

He pointed at her. "You don't have a drink in your hand."

"Oh." She giggled. "I was actually about to fix that."

"Allow me." He gave a mock bow. "What would you like?"

She bit her lip. "I, uh, I'm not sure."

"Well, they have everything here. The good stuff too. What's your favorite drink?"

"I don't really know." She lowered her voice. "I've never actually had a drink. I mean, my parents don't drink at all . . . and, well . . ." She shrugged.

"Oh . . . ?" His eyes lit up. "So you probably want something that tastes sweet, right?"

"I, uh, I guess so."

He nodded. "I know just what you need. Stay right here and I'll be back in a jiff."

She felt nervous as she waited for Brandon. What would her parents say if they knew what she was about to do? Of course, they would never know. And maybe she would simply taste the drink, and hold it in her hand, and pretend like she was a grown-up too. Play their little game.

"Here you go, babe." He handed her what looked like an innocent glass of orange juice.

"I wanted a real drink," she said with disappointment.

"That is a real drink, trust me." He grinned.

"What is it?"

"A screwdriver. Orange juice and vodka."

"Oh?" She took a sniff, and it didn't smell like orange juice usually smelled.

"Go ahead, try it."

She took a cautious sip, and although it didn't taste particularly bad, it didn't taste like regular orange juice either. Unless it was tainted. Surely they wouldn't serve bad orange juice here. It must've been the vodka.

"Like it?" he asked hopefully.

She shrugged. "I guess it's okay." She looked over to see that Todd and Vanessa were still dancing, and she felt fairly certain that her chances with Todd were steadily diminishing. She had to admit that Vanessa looked exceptionally pretty tonight. Wearing a red, sparkly cocktail dress with her hair piled loosely on top of her head, she could easily pass for being in her twenties. No wonder Todd was so taken with her.

"I think Vanessa is getting her Christmas present early this year," Brandon said slyly.

"What?" Although she was pretty sure what he was referring to, she decided to play dumb.

"You know, *Todd*. Vanessa has been trying to bag that boy for years. It looks like tonight is her big night."

"Oh . . ." Lishia took another sip of her drink, then looked away. "Yeah, maybe so."

Now Brandon started rambling about last night's pathetic game and this year's basketball team and how they were so lousy, especially compared to last year's team. "But that's because all the good players were seniors and graduated."

She nodded, pretending to be listening, but she was actually having a hard time focusing—and she felt too warm. "Is it really, really hot in here?" she asked absently.

"Yeah, it's getting pretty stuffy." He took her by the arm. "Let's go out and get some fresh air."

Feeling foggy and slow, she let him lead her outside, where they walked around a bit, and he continued to talk about everything and nothing. Finally they stopped and sat on a garden bench, and the next thing she knew, he was kissing her.

"Hey," she said in a fuzzy-sounding voice, "knock it off."

But he continued trying to hold on to her and kiss her, acting like she liked it, although she did not!

"Hey!" she said more loudly. "I said stop it!" Then she pulled away from him and stumbled back toward the house, letting herself in one of the patio doors. But of course, it felt even hotter in there now. And everything seemed kind of hazy or smoky. She felt very strange. She looked at the nearly empty glass still in her hand and wondered if she could possibly be drunk. *On one drink?* "Must find Riley," she muttered to herself.

Making her way through the crowded, blurry room, she finally found Riley. "I need to go home," she told her in a slurred voice. "I don't feel so good."

Riley peered at her. "Are you drunk?"

"I dunno. I only had one drink . . . I think. I can't remember."

Riley threw back her head and laughed. "You're drunk, Lishia!"

"I'm no drunk—I just don' feel so good. I wanna go home."

"Go sleep it off, Lishia. I'm not ready to leave yet. We're still having fun." She turned to Dayton, probably saying that Lishia was drunk, and now they both started laughing—pointing and laughing.

Lishia didn't know what to do. She looked around the room. Everyone seemed preoccupied, or maybe she had turned invisible. She didn't see Brandon around, but she wasn't about to go outside again in case he was waiting for her. What was wrong with him anyway? More seriously, what was wrong with her?

She went over to where she and Riley had dumped their purses on a bench by the powder room, dug until she found hers, and pulled out her phone. But who could she call? Not her parents—they couldn't see her like this. But she needed someone to help her—and she needed them now.

She went into the powder room and closed the door, trying to focus on the numbers on her phone, but the buttons all blurred together, and then they vanished. When she came to she was on the floor next to the toilet. She picked up her phone again, wondering who to call. Who would help her? She closed her eyes and squeezed the phone to her head, trying to think—and the next thing she knew, her ex–best friend was on the other end, saying, "Lishia? Lishia? What do you want?"

"Janelle?" Lishia was stunned. "Is that really you?"

"Of course it's me. You're the one who called. What do you want, anyway?"

"Oh, Janelle, I need help," Lishia sobbed into the phone.

"What's wrong?"

"I jus' need help." Lishia slumped down onto the floor, pulling her knees up to her chest and clutching the phone to her ear. "Please help me. Help me, Janelle."

"Where are you?"

"Vanesha's housh," she said in a slushy voice. "I'm so sick, and they won't let me go. I need to go . . . and I can't. I need help."

"It's Lishia," Janelle was telling someone else. "I think she's at Vanessa's house, but she sounds like she's drunk. She keeps saying she needs help. But what—"

"Lishia?" Now someone else was talking on the phone.

"Huh?" Lishia let out a sob. "Please help me."

"This is Megan. Are you drunk?"

"I only had one—not even—and I'm sick . . . I feel so sick. Everything is spinning around and around."

"We need to go help her," Megan said loudly. "We're coming, Lishia. Hold on. We'll be there in about fifteen minutes, okay?"

"Oh . . . kay . . ."

"Stay on the phone," Megan told her. "Here, Janelle, you talk to her so I can drive."

"I don't know what to say," Janelle said. "Are you really sick, Lishia? Or is this some twisted little game?"

"I'm sick!" Lishia started to cry now. "Sick."

"Where are you?"

"Vanesha's."

"I know. I mean where in the house are you?"

Lishia looked around the spinning room, shades of gold and green going round and round. "I dunno." She looked at the toilet with what looked like lumpy orange juice floating around in it. Had she thrown up? She tried to remember what this room was called. "Bath . . . room," she finally said as the spinning images turned darker and she slumped over, feeling her forehead clunk against the hard, cold floor . . . and then nothing.

fourteen

"Come on," Megan said loudly. "Let's get her out of here."

Lishia looked up to see Janelle and Megan. They were tugging on her arms, and Chelsea was behind them. "Come on, stand up," Janelle told her.

Lishia's legs felt rubbery. "I am st-st-standing."

"Come on," Megan said. "Let's move it."

All three of them pushed, pulled, and tugged to get Lishia out of the house. As they left there were a lot of curious faces watching and people making comments, saying things like how people shouldn't drink too much and make fools of themselves.

"I jus' had one," Lishia slurred back at them. "Jus' one. Tha's all."

"Yeah, right," Janelle said once they were outside. "If you only had one, it must've been supersized."

"Or maybe just one bottle," Megan said.

"At least she threw up," Chelsea said as they helped Lishia

into the back of Megan's car, where she slumped down into the seat. "That should help some."

"Hopefully she won't throw up again," Janelle said.

"I'll sit with her," Chelsea offered.

"Don't let her throw up in my car," Megan said.

Their voices continued to bounce around in the car. Sometimes Lishia caught their words; sometimes they floated right past. But one thing they all agreed on was that she was drunk.

"I think we should take her to the emergency room," Chelsea said.

"What can they do for her there?" Janelle asked.

"Make sure she's okay," Chelsea said.

"Really?" Megan sounded unsure. "Should I take her to the hospital?"

"No." Lishia sat up and rubbed her aching head. "No hospital. No, no, no."

"Take her home," Janelle said. "Let her parents decide."

"No, no, no," Lishia said again. "Please, don't take me home."

"How much did you really drink?" Janelle demanded.

"I dunno . . ." Lishia tried to think. "Jus' one. Orange juice . . . and something."

"What kind of something?" Megan asked.

"I dunno." Lishia took a deep breath, willing herself to feel better. She did not want them taking her to the hospital—or home. "I'm gonna be okay," she said in a shaky voice.

"I'm so disappointed in you," Janelle said. "It's like you've turned into someone else, Lishia. Why?"

Lishia sighed. "I dunno."

"I'll tell you why," Janelle said. "Because you've turned your back on God, Lishia. And look where it got you."

Lishia started to cry. She knew Janelle was right, but why did she have to be so mean about it? "You turned your back on me," she said quietly.

"What?"

"I said you turned your back on me." Lishia turned to face Chelsea. "You tossed me aside for her."

Chelsea looked sad. "I'm sorry," she said gently. "Is that how you feel?"

"Uh-huh." Lishia sniffed.

"I thought you were the one who turned your back on Janelle," she said.

"I thought so too," Janelle said sharply. "Every time I asked you to do something you refused, Lishia. You shoved me away and you know it."

Lishia started to cry harder now. "I did not."

"Yes, you did. You were always—"

"Stop it," Chelsea said. "Don't pick on poor Lishia, Janelle. Don't you think she's been through enough for one night? Be nice to her."

"Chelsea's right," Megan said gently. "Lishia called us for help. Not to get lectured, Janelle."

"Are you feeling any better?" Chelsea asked.

Lishia shrugged. "Maybe."

"Let's stop at 7-Eleven and get her some soda to drink," Chelsea suggested. "That might make her feel better. Then we can decide what to do next."

"Don't take me home like this," Lishia pleaded.

They sat in the 7-Eleven parking lot, sipping on sodas and discussing Lishia's fate.

"Lishia can spend the night at my house," Megan offered. "I mean, if we're sure she's going to be okay."

"I'm going to be okay." Lishia took another slow sip. "I feel better already."

"I'm still curious about how much you had to drink," Janelle said. "I don't want to be mean, but it's hard to believe one drink could've done that."

"Do you think anyone could've tampered with your drink?" Megan said suddenly. "I've heard that some guys use that date rape drug and—"

"Oh, that's ridiculous," Janelle said. "You saw the party. Vanessa's parents were there and everything—"

"Yeah, and I have to say that was pretty weird," Chelsea said. "What kind of parents let their kids have a party like that?"

"Unfortunately, there are lots of parents who think that's okay," Megan said.

"Not mine," Lishia said sadly.

"Speaking of parents, it's nearly my curfew," Megan said. "I need to get you guys home."

"But I can stay with you?" Lishia asked hopefully.

"As long as you're sure you're okay. I don't want to have to take you to the ER in the middle of the night. My mom would freak."

"I feel a lot better." Lishia sighed. "Thank you, guys, for helping me. I don't know what I would've done without you. I was so out of it, I barely remember calling Janelle."

"Yeah, I was pretty surprised to see it was you on the phone," Janelle admitted. "We were just leaving youth group, and I had just turned my phone on and it was ringing."

"I think it was a God thing," Megan said. "I've been praying for you, Lishia. Even tonight, when we broke into small groups to pray, I asked everyone to pray for you. I thought you were going through something hard."

"Thanks," Lishia muttered, trying not to cry again. Megan had no idea.

"Well, I hope you learned a lesson," Janelle said a bit sharply.

"Janelle." Chelsea had a warning in her voice. "Lighten up, okay?"

"It's only because I care about her," Janelle said defensively.

"Well, try to care a little more gently," Megan suggested.

Megan and Lishia made it into Megan's house a little before midnight. "My mom and sister have probably gone to bed," Megan whispered as she grabbed some snacks from the kitchen. "Just be quiet on the stairs."

Soon they were safely tucked away in Megan's room, munching on junk food, which was surprisingly soothing to Lishia's stomach. "You know," Lishia said as she crunched on tortilla chips, "I was wondering about what you said about that date rape drug." She told Megan about Brandon getting her drink for her and how he was quick to take her outside and begin putting the move on her. "Almost like he knew what was up."

"Seriously?" Megan looked alarmed. "You think he slipped you something?"

"Well, he sure disappeared fast—I mean, after I started feeling bad and told him to leave me alone. I never saw him after I went back in the house to get help. It's like he took off. And I swear to you, Megan, I only had that one drink." She then confessed as to why she even did that. "But I will never, never do that again. I swear I never want another alcoholic beverage in my life."

Megan laughed. "I guess that's one way to stay on the wagon."

"I can't believe what a mess I've made of my life." Lishia felt tears coming again.

"Oh, it's not that bad," Megan assured her. "At least you figured out that you're not into drinking."

"No, my life is a lot worse than what happened tonight, Megan. Trust me, it's really a great, big, messed-up mess." Now she started to cry.

"Why?" Megan asked. "What's wrong?"

"Everything," she sobbed.

"Are you pregnant?"

Lishia stared at Megan in disbelief. "No way—of course not."

"Oh, well, you made it sound so bad . . . I just figured."

"I guess the only good thing about my life is that I am not pregnant." Despite herself, Lishia smiled.

"So what is it that's so terrible?"

"I feel like I sold my soul to the devil."

"Huh?" Megan reached for a cheese curl.

"And the devil's name is Riley Atkins."

"Oh . . ."

"Can I trust you, Megan?"

"Absolutely."

And so, for the first time since Lishia got sucked into Riley's twisted world of schemes and scams, Lishia began to tell the whole ugly story. By the time she finished, she could tell that Megan was truly shocked.

"So, let me get this straight." Megan's brow was creased. "Riley tampered with the votes so the real alternate cheerleader was knocked out of the running and you'd replace Gillian?"

Lishia nodded. "Michelle really won. Riley told me Michelle

would've been disqualified anyway, although I'm not so sure that wasn't just another one of her lies."

"And Riley got Todd's party busted so Gillian would get arrested?"

"She told me she left early and called from a pay phone."

"But how did she know Gillian would still be there and intoxicated?"

"Because Gillian was totally wasted, and she'd been thrown in the pool. I suppose Riley knew she'd gone upstairs to get out of her wet clothes."

"And she did all this just because Gillian was going out with Dayton?"

"It seems extreme, I know. Especially considering Dayton hadn't really been that into Gillian." Lishia shook her head. "The more I get to know Riley, the more I think she does things like this because she is mean—just plain mean."

"She's always been pretty manipulative," Megan said. "Remember the time she tricked Janelle into doing her homework for a month back in sixth grade?"

"Now that you mention it . . ."

"I tried to warn you a few times."

"I know, but it was already too late by then. Riley's been holding stuff over my head almost from the get-go. It's like she had it all planned out, how she'd blackmail me and keep me under her thumb. When I questioned her on it, she actually threatened to tell Mrs. Glassman that I was the one behind everything. You have to admit, it makes sense. I mean, why should Riley go to all that trouble for me? She already had her place on the squad. It would be totally believable that I had schemed this all up. She could even say that up until recently, she and I hadn't even been friends. So why would she go to so much effort—just for me?"

"I'll tell you why she went to so much effort, Lishia. She wanted to own you."

"But why?"

"Because she wanted a best friend she could totally control."

"And she got one, all right." Lishia wiped her nose on a paper napkin. "I am such a pathetic wimp. I let her reel me in."

"Why do you think she went after you?" Megan peered curiously at her.

"Because she knew I was such a pathetic wimp?"

Megan smiled. "I think it's because she knew you'd make a really good friend. Because you're loyal and trustworthy. And I'm sure on some nicer level, if she has any such thing, it's what Riley wanted too. The problem is, that girl is too messed up to know what to do with a truly good friend."

"What am I going to do, Megan?"

Megan's expression grew serious. "You have to come clean."

Lishia groaned. "Coming clean will mean everyone will know how totally filthy I really am." Lishia felt a hard lump growing in her throat. "My parents have been so proud of me, even my grandma. And I actually had fun cheering at our first game and being with Amanda. She's so sweet. Was that game really just last night? It seems like a month ago."

"You've been through a lot tonight." Megan yawned.

"And I put you through a lot too." Lishia shook her head. "I'm sorry to drag you through all my mud."

"It's okay. I think it's actually kind of exciting to be involved in this."

"You mean my big, fat, messed-up life?"

"I mean helping you put it back together again. Because

you must know you have to fix this, Lishia. You have to get your heart right with God again."

Lishia closed her eyes, leaned her head back, and wished she could turn back the clock. "The truth is, I can hardly stand to imagine what God thinks of me now."

"God hasn't changed, Lishia. He still loves you. He always has. He always will. He wants you to come to him and confess everything—kind of like you just did with me—and then he wants to forgive you and give you that clean slate you're wanting."

Lishia opened her eyes and let out a long, tired sigh. "I wish it was that simple, Megan."

"It is that simple. Tell him you're sorry, and he'll help you straighten things out."

"I would . . . but at the moment I'm so exhausted I can barely think straight."

"Yeah, me too. But if you want to pray before you go to sleep, I'm willing to pray with you." Megan gave a hopeful smile.

"I . . . uh . . . I don't think I'm ready for that quite yet. I mean, when I get my heart right with God—and I plan to—well, I want to do it right. I want to be 100 percent sincere. I don't think I can do that right now. Okay?"

"Okay . . . if you're sure."

She nodded. "I'm sure. I'll do it later."

However, instead of falling asleep, Lishia was still wide awake an hour or more later. So much was running through her head—almost like she was in hyper-mode. Mostly she was trying to figure an easy way out of her big, fat mess—a nice, neat way she could escape Riley and public humiliation at the same time. She imagined a scenario where she would get evidence about Riley breaking the code of conduct and then blackmail Riley to get her to back off. But then she realized she would simply be imitating Riley—and she didn't want to stoop that low. She considered gathering evidence and turning in all the cheerleaders, including herself, so that everyone on the squad (well, except Amanda) would be disciplined, but that seemed mean-spirited and spiteful.

After she had exhausted every escape scenario, she thought back to earlier that evening and how that horrible drink had made her so sick. The more she thought about it, the more she believed that Brandon—or someone very vile—really had slipped something into her drink. What else could it have been? Unless there had been something wrong with the orange juice . . . and that seemed ridiculous. But if Brandon really had spiked her drink, what could she even do about it? Any attempt to report what he'd done—and who would she tell?—would simply reveal that she'd put herself in a compromising position by drinking alcohol, which was also in direct violation of the conduct code and would get her suspended from cheerleading. Besides, what proof would she have that Brandon had actually done anything? Wouldn't it simply be her word against his? And what if he was innocent?

Her head was throbbing again—nearly as badly as it had hurt earlier. She wasn't sure if this was an aftereffect of her drinking experience or simply the result of the way she was beating her head against this imaginary wall.

She could hear Megan sleeping peacefully in the bed on the other side of the room. Lishia tried to remember the last time she'd slept soundly like that—relaxed and guilt free. Would she ever be able to sleep like that again?

She wondered if she'd been a fool to confess all to Megan.

Sure, Megan had promised to keep her secret, but Lishia knew from personal experience that friends (even the ones who profess to be your "best" friend) can be flaky. What if Megan decided the right thing to do (if Lishia didn't confess) would be to tell on her? Could Lishia really trust Megan? For that matter, could she really trust anyone? It seemed that every which way she turned, someone was trying to undermine her, stabbing her in the back, taking advantage. Really, besides her parents (who would be furious at her if they knew the truth), she could trust no one!

fifteen

Time to get up," Megan said cheerfully.

"I can't open my eyes," Lishia said in a gruff voice. "Barely got to sleep . . . need a couple more hours . . . exhausted."

"My mom says anyone in this house has to go to church. Unless they're sick, that is."

"I am sick." She moaned and rolled over, facing the wall.

"Really?" Megan sounded a little concerned. "Do you think you're still messed up from last night?"

"I don't know . . . but I know I can't make it to church. Go without me. *Please.*"

"Okay . . . but my mom won't like it."

"Tell her I'm sick, Megan. Really, truly sick. I'm sorry."

After a while, Lishia heard their car leaving and forced herself to get up. She needed to get herself cleaned up and out of here. Maybe she could get home while her parents were still at church. She took a quick shower, then borrowed some of Megan's clothes, which were a little big but better than the ruined cocktail dress and messed-up shoes that she stuffed into a grocery bag. Hopefully she could figure out a way to clean them and return them to Riley.

Megan's house was about a ten-minute walk from Lishia's, but each step was accompanied by an agonizing throb inside her head. Whatever she'd had last night was still making her feel lousy today.

It wasn't until she got home and into her room that she checked her phone. Of course, she had about a dozen text messages, mostly from Riley but a few from Vanessa. Both girls were mad at her, but Vanessa's sounded seriously angry.

Lishia was about to put her phone away when it rang. Thinking it would be Riley and that Lishia would need to explain some things, she answered without even looking. It was Vanessa.

"So you're still alive," Vanessa said in a snarky tone. "Too bad."

"Thanks for caring."

"You're right, I don't care about you, Lishia. And I can't believe how you ruined last night's party."

"I ruined the party?" Lishia figured Vanessa was being overly dramatic. "How so?"

"How so? I cannot believe you would act like that at my parents' Christmas party. Well, I'm sorry, but it's unforgivable."

"*Unforgivable?*" Lishia felt indignant. "Do you honestly think I had any control over that or that I did it on purpose?"

"I have no idea what you did or why. But everyone got very worried when your stupid friends showed up like gangbusters, acting like they thought we were holding you against your will. Then you were so out of it that they had to practically drag you out like some kind of skid row bum. It was so embarrassing. If I were you, I'd never show my face in public again."

"But I—"

"Seriously, Lishia, if you can't hold your alcohol, don't drink!"

"I didn't even have one whole drink."

"Yeah, right. You were totally wasted, Lishia! I know this for a fact because I had to clean up the nasty mess you made in our powder room. Ugh, I don't even want to think about it."

"I—I'm sorry about that, but honestly, I didn't have more than one drink. I'm convinced someone slipped something into my drink—maybe even Brandon because he was right there and—"

"Oh, Lishia, don't be ridiculous. I've known Brandon my whole life, and he would never do something that sleazy. Besides, it was my parents' Christmas party with no lowlife losers in attendance. Well, except for you and your pathetic stunt. You managed to bring the party straight down."

"It wasn't my fault. Honestly, I'm certain I was drugged," Lishia insisted. "Maybe it was a date rape drug or—"

"You are starting to sound just like Gillian Rodowski now." Vanessa's voice dripped with disgust. "You know, I hope you get kicked off the squad like she did. You really don't deserve to be a cheerleader, Lishia. Not after what you pulled last night. Did you know that your friends were all laughing at you after you were gone? You were a complete embarrassment to yourself and everyone associated with you. And thanks to you, my mom is saying I can't invite my friends to their parties. All because of your total ignorance."

"Well, maybe that's a good thing," Lishia said meekly.

"Maybe kids shouldn't be invited to your parents' drinking parties."

"It figures you would say something that stupid. You know, I didn't even want to invite you to the party in the first place—that was all Riley's idea. She insisted you should be there, and like an idiot, I agreed to let you come. Well, look where that got me."

"I said I'm sorry."

"Well, from now on consider yourself uninvited from any event that has anything to do with my life!" The line went dead.

Lishia closed her phone and sighed. Could her life get any worse? Thanks to Riley, it could. Wearing a furious expression, Riley showed up at Lishia's house just as Lishia's parents got home from church. Lishia waved at her parents in the driveway, then tugged Riley inside.

"Don't say a word about this," Lishia told her as she led her to her bedroom.

"What on earth was wrong with you last night?" Riley demanded as Lishia closed the door.

Once again, Lishia attempted to tell the true story, even accusing Brandon of being the culprit. "It wasn't my fault."

"I cannot believe you're blaming poor Brandon for your outrageous behavior," Riley said. "Especially after he told me how he tried to help you, how he encouraged you to slow down the drinking. He was worried you were overdoing it—and just because you were jealous over Todd." She rolled her eyes. "So pathetic."

"You have got to be kidding. That's what Brandon told you?"

Riley pointed at the shoes and dress from last night, heaped in a corner of the floor like a pile of garbage. "My Marc Jacobs shoes!" She picked up a heel, then made a disgusted face as she dropped it back down. "And my dress!" She glared at Lishia. "I can't believe I thought you were my friend," she said in an icy tone. "This is how you thank me? You get so wasted that you barf all over my good clothes? You are unbelievable!"

Lishia held up her hands. "I'm sorry about your stuff . . . but really, it wasn't my fault."

"No." Riley walked toward the door. "I suppose it was my fault. *Right?*"

"I didn't say that." Lishia didn't know what to say. And her head was still throbbing. Maybe this was all for the best. Maybe this was how she could shake Riley out of her life, once and for all.

"Maybe it's time for you to put on your big girl pants." With one hand on the door, Riley looked haughtily at Lishia. "Take some personal responsibility and own up to your mistakes."

Lishia didn't try to hide her surprise. "Really, I should take responsibility and own up to my mistakes? That's very interesting . . . coming from you."

Riley gave her a completely innocent look. "Whatever do you mean?"

"You know exactly what I mean." Lishia narrowed her eyes.

Riley arched one eyebrow. "What are you suggesting?"

Lishia honestly did not know what she was suggesting. It wasn't as if she thought she could threaten Riley. Seriously, that would be like playing with fire—Lishia could end up even more burned than she was right now.

"Well . . . ?" Riley's tone was pure impatience.

"What do you want from me?" Lishia asked her. "I mean, seriously, Riley, what is it that you expect from me? Do you just want me to be your puppet? You pull the strings and I do what you want?"

Riley shrugged. "Excuse me, but I thought we were friends, Lishia."

"Friends . . ."

"Unfortunately, you keep disappointing me. And I have to say that these little tantrums and your moodiness, well, it gets a little old. Seriously, that's not how I expect my friends to act."

"How do you expect your friends to act?" Lishia was trying to keep the disdain out of her voice, but it wasn't easy.

"Like friends." Riley's mouth formed a smile, but her eyes were cold. "We are still friends, aren't we?"

Lishia didn't say anything.

Now Riley's smile vanished. "I do so much for you, Lishia. And in the end, you are so unappreciative. You know, I'm starting to think that you are really high maintenance."

If Lishia wasn't so angry—and hurt—she might've laughed at that one. *She* was high maintenance? What about Riley?

"Here is what I expect, Lishia." Riley still had her hand on the doorknob. "I expect you to get it together. I mean, you look like a pathetic mess, and I would be totally embarrassed to be seen with you right now. By tomorrow, you better pull yourself together. I expect you to be back in top form when I pick you up for school in the morning." She made that fake-looking smile again. "Okay?"

Lishia didn't answer as she stared in wonder. What was it with Riley? But Riley seemed oblivious, simply exiting the room like she thought she was the reigning queen. Maybe she was—at least when it came to Lishia's life. And maybe

Lishia deserved to be ruled over like that. It wasn't as if she had been doing a great job of running her life anyway.

✢

Lishia did what Riley told her to do. She cleaned herself up, put on her happy cheerleader face, and for the next couple of days "ate crow" while all her so-called cheerleader friends made jokes at her expense. She pretended to take the teasing in stride and hoped that Vanessa would eventually get over it. But even Amanda seemed to hold Lishia at arm's length now, as if she were disappointed in her. By midweek, Lishia considered switching allegiance back to her old friends—the ones who had rescued her from Vanessa's on Saturday night. In many ways it would be a whole lot easier.

Except for one thing: she knew they would want her to come clean and to get her heart right with God. At least Megan would. Now that Megan knew all the dirty little details of Lishia's messed-up life, she would expect Lishia to confess her sins and turn back to God. But that would mean confessing everything to everyone, and that would be a public humiliation far worse than what Vanessa and the others were dishing out. And the sad truth was that Lishia was simply not ready for it.

But every time Lishia ran into Megan—and she was trying to avoid her—she could read the words written across Megan's face: *When are you going to make this thing right?* So Lishia tried even harder not to cross paths with her. Fortunately, it was just a few days until winter break. For some unexplainable reason, Lishia thought she might have enough time to figure things out during the holidays. At least that's what she kept telling herself. Just two more days of school, one more basketball game, and then she would take a nice long break and see if there was some way to fix this mess—or move to a different school.

The one bright spot of her week, if she could call it that, was when Gillian approached her on Wednesday morning. At first Lishia wasn't sure whether to run or even scream when Gillian cornered her in the nearly deserted locker bay.

"Don't look so scared," Gillian said.

"I'm not scared," Lishia lied as she held her books between her and Gillian.

"I want to apologize to you," Gillian said in a slightly gruff voice. "Just so you know, I'm doing this because it's part of my twelve-step program. And because I realize now that I've been trying to blame you for all the times I messed up. But I know it's not really your fault." She sighed. "It's mine. So I want to say sorry. Okay?"

"Okay." Lishia nodded. "Thanks. I appreciate that."

"Yeah." Then Gillian turned and walked away. Just like that. Lishia didn't even want her to go. She actually wanted to talk some more, although she had no idea what she would say.

For the rest of the day, Lishia tried to wrap her head around that surprising apology. It didn't quite make sense. Especially when Lishia knew that she owed Gillian an even bigger apology. But how was she supposed to do that? And now that Gillian was owning up to some of her own problems—and she really had had some problems—maybe Lishia's involvement in the whole thing was minor in comparison. Or maybe Lishia was just fooling herself . . . again. Mostly she didn't want to think about it right now. All she wanted was to get through the next few days. Then she would try to think about everything. And she would try to come up with some kind of an escape plan.

But by Friday, she was getting worried. It was so easy to slip back into the old routine of lies and games and being manipulated and frustrated and then feeling guilty all over again. What if this became her permanent state of being? Could she even stand herself? Could she stand the alternative? Confessing the truth would mean that the whole world would see what a dirty rotten person she truly was. How could she possibly bear that kind of condemnation?

On Friday, Lishia was walking around the school, wearing the crisp purple-and-white cheerleader outfit, which most of the smell had been eradicated from, and she could see that some kids (though not all) looked at her with a degree of respect. She liked that. Did she deserve it? Well, no . . . but did anyone?

"Are you enjoying being a cheerleader?"

Lishia looked up from where she was washing her hands to see Michelle Parkington gazing at her in the mirror. "I guess so." Lishia forced a weak smile.

"You look great in the uniform."

Lishia locked eyes with Michelle and without even thinking, spoke her mind. "Do you wish it was you instead of me?"

Michelle pushed a long strand of dark hair over her shoulder. "I did at first . . . but I'm okay."

Lishia dried her hands, ready to leave, wishing she hadn't asked.

"Amanda really thought I was first alternate," Michelle said wistfully. "I suppose that got my hopes up. And everyone thought I did pretty good last spring at tryouts. But I guess they were wrong."

"Would you have been able to do it—I mean, if you really had been first alternate? Would you have qualified for cheerleading?"

Michelle's brow creased. "Sure, why not?"

Lishia shrugged.

"Anyway, you looked pretty good at your first game." She giggled. "Well, a lot better than you did at the pep assembly, that is."

"Ugh, don't remind me. I was terrible last week."

"I'm sure it'll get easier for you," Michelle said kindly. "Just give it time."

Lishia wanted to question Michelle further, to find out why there had been rumors going around that she had problems and that she never would've made the cut. But then Lishia remembered who told her those things to start with: Riley, the one who pulled all the strings. Naturally, she could spin a story any way she liked. Whatever suited her agenda—and she always had one.

"Ready for practice?" Riley asked her as they met in the locker bay to get their coats. The cheerleaders were having a last-minute practice to work on the dance routine after Amanda had changed some moves.

"Sure." Lishia made her usual smile, which was feeling more and more plastic.

"It's nice to see you made such a solid comeback this week," Riley said as they walked to the girls' gym. "I told you the teasing would subside after a day or two . . . If you ignore that stuff, it usually goes away."

"Well, I still find it hard to ignore Brandon." Lishia could hear the bitter edge in her voice. But that was because someone in art class had made a derogatory comment today, warning her to watch her alcohol intake after the game tonight. Sure, she had laughed it off. But then the girl had acted pseudo-sympathetic, insinuating that Lishia had gotten wasted to get Todd's attention.

"What's up with Brandon now?" Riley asked with irritation.

"It's the way he spread those lies about me. I mean, he knew exactly what was going on that night, and then he goes and makes this crud up."

"He's just trying to get attention." Riley looked irritated now.

"It's a pretty disgusting way to get attention." She frowned at Riley. "And I have to say, it's a little disturbing that you still consider him your friend."

"Oh, Brandon is harmless."

"Harmless?" Lishia felt her anger rising again. "He goes around telling everyone that I stole a bottle of Vanessa's parents' vodka, stashed it in my purse, then took it outside and drank the whole thing just to get over Todd."

Riley laughed. "No one really believes all that, Lishia."

"But why did he say it? It's a bald-faced lie."

"Brandon's just a clown. Like I said, he thrives on attention. So he spins a silly tale. Big deal."

"Would it be a big deal if he spun a tale like that about *you*?"

Riley's mouth twisted to one side. "Come on, Lishia. You need to learn to stop taking everything so seriously. You need to laugh at yourself more. Lighten up, girlfriend."

Lishia wanted to point out that Riley never laughed at herself, but they were entering the gym now. Time to put on her happy cheerleader act again, but Lishia could tell it was all wearing a bit thin. More and more, she felt like a pot was bubbling inside of her, like someday it was going to boil over and burn everyone and everything anywhere near it. How could she keep up this act?

sixteen

Lishia knew better than to complain about her position in the pyramid at halftime—always at the bottom, even though she was one of the smaller girls. She knew it was purely symbolic. So she would bend over and bear the weight of the other cheerleaders, their feet and knees digging into her back and shoulders, and smile with gritted teeth. She didn't complain because she felt it was what she deserved. Even so, she did not believe she deserved to be bullied by Riley. Really, a girl could only take so much.

Toward the end of the basketball game, Lishia had reached her limit with her so-called best friend. It was like Riley kept pushing her, nagging her, and belittling her—as if it was a game and she wanted to see how much Lishia could take.

"That's enough," Lishia said finally.

"What?" Riley blinked innocently. "What's wrong?"

"I'm sick of being bossed by you, Riley. Stop telling me what to do. I'm not your puppet."

Riley laughed.

"I mean it." Lishia narrowed her eyes. "Back off!" She moved herself to the other end of the lineup, taking a place beside Krista, who tossed her a questioning look but went on cheering just the same.

"I needed a break from Riley," she quietly told Krista between cheers.

Krista gave her a knowing nod. For the rest of the game, Lishia enjoyed a much more peaceful position in the lineup. However, she knew Riley would be mad because she was on the end now—and Riley hated being on the end. If she had her way, she'd be in the middle.

As soon as the game ended (another loss), Lishia pulled out her phone and called Mom, hoping to get a ride home. But her call went straight to voice mail. Instead of leaving a message, she hung up. Fearing that Riley was heading her way and probably on the warpath, Lishia streaked off toward the bathroom, hoping to get lost in the crowd, which wasn't easy considering her purple-and-white uniform.

"What's your hurry?"

Lishia looked over her shoulder to see Gillian peering curiously at her. Lishia had just cut in front of her in the bathroom line. "Sorry," she said. "Were you waiting for the restroom?" There were at least a dozen standing outside the bathroom, probably at least that many inside. Really, it was hopeless.

"No, I was just trying to get out of here."

"Me too," Lishia said suddenly, pushing her way through the line and walking with Gillian. She had no idea why she was doing this or where she was going, but it felt like a good escape.

"Where's Riley?" Gillian asked as they exited the building

with a bunch of others. "I thought you two were connected at the hip."

Lishia grimaced. "I was actually running away from her." She couldn't believe she'd just admitted that to Gillian—considering everything, it seemed like a slightly irrational thing to do. But maybe that was what anger did to a person.

Gillian threw back her head and laughed. Her eyes twinkled and her ponytail shook. She had on her letterman jacket, and if one didn't look too closely, she could easily be confused with a cheerleader.

"So, how are you doing?" Lishia asked in a friendly voice.

"Just great." Gillian rolled her eyes as her tone grew sarcastic. "Life is just peachy. I go to treatment, make amends. Lovely."

"Sorry. If it makes you feel any better, I would gladly trade places with you."

Gillian looked skeptical. "Yeah, right. I'll bet you would."

"I honestly think I would," Lishia admitted.

"Well, I know the cheerleader games and politics can be a nasty little rat race sometimes," Gillian admitted. "I guess I don't miss that."

"Hey," Lishia glanced over her shoulder. "Do you have time to talk?"

"I thought we *were* talking."

Lishia's eyes darted from side to side, hoping that Riley or the others hadn't spotted her with Gillian. "Do you have a car?"

"Sure."

"Can you give me a ride?"

"I'm not going to Allegro's, if that's what you mean." Gillian firmly shook her head. "I'm not ready for that yet."

"I'm not either. How about we go grab a coffee or soda or something?"

Gillian looked suspicious now. "Why?"

"There's something important I need to ask you about, okay? It's kind of private."

She shrugged. "I guess I don't have anything to lose—not anymore, anyway."

As soon as they were in the car, Lishia began to apologize. It all came jumbling out in a slightly incoherent way. "I was so rude to you that night at the party. I still feel bad that you got kicked off . . . and that I took your place." She looked down at her uniform. "I even felt bad when our moms did the deal on your uniform. Really, you have no idea how guilty I've felt about all of that."

"I know it's not really your fault," Gillian assured her. "I mean, I was pretty mad at you too. But like I already told you, I know I acted as bad as you did. Probably worse. The truth is, I don't even remember everything from that stupid party. I was pretty out of it that night. But I do know this—and it's from going to my treatment meetings—I know I'm supposed to clean the slate. I've been trying to tell everyone that I'm sorry for the crud I pulled. Like I told you the other day, I'm sorry for how I treated you."

"But I want you to know that I really am sorry," Lishia said firmly. "If I could go back and do that all differently, I would."

"So . . . now I'm curious . . . why *did* you start going after me back then?" Gillian asked. "I mean, I realize I was a brat sometimes, but it's not like we'd ever had problems before. It was like you suddenly hated me."

"Riley."

"Oh?"

"She wanted me to act like that. And I needed a friend." Lishia felt embarrassed to admit this. "Somehow Riley made me believe that you had been going after her, like you were trying to make her life miserable. And I stupidly bought into it. I wanted to be friends with her . . . so I suppose I made myself believe her."

"She can be convincing when she wants to be."

"So I've seen."

"And I suspected that she was feeling jealous about Dayton and me. She didn't come out and say as much, but suddenly we were squabbling over stupid little things. I figured it was her usual passive-aggressive routine."

"Passive-aggressive?" Lishia was feeling a little nervous now. How much did she plan to tell Gillian about Riley? What if she was getting in over her head? Maybe she should shut her mouth before it was too late.

"Well, I've known Riley for a long time, and I'm well aware of how she works people. In my opinion she has a passive-aggressive personality. I know all about that because my dad has it—that's why my parents divorced. Anyway, I know Riley is a major manipulator, so I can imagine how she might've manipulated you."

"There's no denying that Riley goes for what she wants." Lishia sighed. "And God help anyone who gets in her way."

"Tell me about it." Gillian shook her head.

"Now all I want is to escape her." The handle of her bag was twisted tightly in her hands. "Seriously, I need a Riley break."

"So was that what you wanted to talk about?" Gillian asked as she parked at a diner. "That whole thing with Riley?"

"Actually, there's a little more to it." Lishia took in a deep breath as they got out of the car.

"What kind of more?"

Lishia felt a wave of fear rush through her. What was she doing talking to Gillian like this? Riley would go for serious revenge if she knew who Lishia was with right now. And who knew what Riley was capable of? She could smear Lishia's reputation at cyberspeed, and Lishia knew she would. Beyond that, Lishia would be kicked off the squad, she might even be suspended from school, and everyone in the community would know she was a fraud—including her parents.

But that wasn't all that was at stake. If Lishia spilled the beans with Gillian, there was no telling what Gillian might do. Naturally, she'd be furious—and with just cause. Perhaps even worse than that, she would be hurt, and just when Lishia was starting to feel like they could almost be friends, like they shared some commonalities. But seriously, what kind of friend could Lishia be to Gillian? Or anyone for that matter? Lishia was a loser and a fraud—and her life would completely unravel if she let this wildcat out of the bag.

As they were seated in a booth, she wished she'd thought this through a little better. To continue this conversation with Gillian was self destructive to say the least. But Lishia felt so bone tired as the waitress handed her a greasy menu—like she'd been running an unending marathon of madness. Maybe this was the only way to end this thing.

seventeen

Lishia couldn't believe what she was doing and who she was with, but she followed Gillian's lead by ordering the chocolate cream pie and coffee. Then, bracing herself for the fallout that was sure to come, she decided to continue this conversation. But first she wanted to tell Gillian about her own experience at Vanessa's party last week. It was only a hunch, but she suspected that Gillian might relate to it . . . a lot. So she explained about feeling out of place and deciding to take the plunge and try her first taste of alcohol. "Of course, it turned out to be the stupidest move of my life . . . or nearly." She grimaced to think of how many stupid things she'd done in the past few weeks—the list was overwhelming.

"Oh, yeah, I heard about that at school." Gillian chuckled. "I was kind of surprised that you'd get wasted like that—and for a guy too." She shook her head. "Too bad."

"But the thing is, I didn't get wasted. I only had one drink." She held up a finger. "And I don't think I even drank the whole thing—although I can't remember it all too clearly."

Gillian looked slightly curious as the waitress set down their pies and coffees. "Really?"

"Brandon Procter got the drink for me." Lishia watched Gillian's eyes flicker slightly, almost as if this triggered something.

"Brandon Procter?" Her brows lifted.

"Yes, and I honestly believe he slipped something into it," Lishia confided.

"Really?" She leaned forward with interest.

"Vanessa mentioned that you thought something like that might've happened to you at Todd's birthday party."

Gillian nodded as she slowly picked up her fork. "Uh-huh."

"Are you willing to talk about it?"

"I guess so . . . but I have to admit, it's pretty foggy. I mean, it's been a while, and I was pretty out of it."

"That's okay. Just tell me what you remember."

Gillian began to tell about how she suddenly felt completely intoxicated. "But the weird thing was, I'd only had one, maybe two drinks. And it's not like I never drank before . . . not like some people." She gave a mischievous grin. "In fact, that's what makes it tricky . . . because there were some other times when I drank too much, and I felt similar. Not nearly so sick, though."

"I'm curious . . . were you around Brandon that night?"

"Not really. I mean, he was around—you know the way Brandon can be all over the place, buzzing around like a pesky mosquito. But I don't know that I actually spoke to him or anything." Her mouth twisted to one side. "As I recall he was buzzing around Riley a lot—you know, before she and Dayton decided to get back together. Maybe Brandon thought he had a chance with her." She laughed. "I think they'd make a good couple!"

Lishia laughed, then suddenly stopped. "Now that you mention it, I do remember Brandon being around Riley that night too."

"Uh-huh." Gillian took a big bite of whipped cream. "So?"

The wheels in Lishia's mind were spinning faster now. What if Riley had something to do with Gillian being inebriated? After all, it was Riley who'd blown the whistle on the drinking party, running before the police arrived. And Riley had known Gillian would be caught there. What if the whole thing was Riley's elaborate setup all along? "So I'm curious . . . did anyone check your alcohol level at the police station?"

Gillian shrugged. "Yeah, sure, they took some blood. I think I even told them I'd been drugged. I haven't heard back what the numbers were or anything, but I do have a lawyer working on it."

"It would be interesting to know the results . . . I mean, if someone really slipped you something . . . wouldn't you want to know?"

"Now that you mention it, I guess I would, although I've been trying to accept responsibility for the bad choices I made. To recover, you have to admit that you were the one who blew it. You can't keep blaming everyone else."

Lishia nodded. "Yes, I can understand that. But what if someone helped you to blow it?"

Gillian frowned as she set down her fork. "What do you mean exactly?"

"I'm not sure, but I am curious."

"Can you be more specific?"

Lishia took a deep breath. "Riley will kill me."

"Huh?"

Lishia swallowed hard. "I don't know where to begin . . ."

"Just begin," Gillian commanded.

Lishia decided to start by focusing on that night of Todd's birthday party. "I already told you about how Riley was trying to get me to go after you, but now I think there was even more going on." She spilled out the story of how Riley left the party and called the police.

"What?" Gillian's eyes were full of anger.

"I know. I was mad too. I was still there when the cops arrived. Todd and I made a run for it. But now I'm thinking about how Riley told me she left the party right after you were thrown in the pool. Do you recall who initiated the pool incident?"

Gillian looked confused. "Not exactly."

"It was Brandon."

She nodded like that made sense. "Do you think Riley put him up to it? Like he was her puppet?"

"I don't know . . . but I guess it wouldn't surprise me."

"So she set the whole thing up just to get me. She got Brandon to slip something into my drink. Then she told her little minion to throw me in the pool. And knowing full well that I'd get caught like that, she ran out to call the police?"

"I never thought about it like that until tonight, Gillian. But I have to admit it all adds up."

"Why are you telling me this?" Gillian's eyes narrowed. "Is this another one of Riley's setups?"

"No, of course not. If anything, I'm putting myself in a really bad place with Riley now. When she hears that I've told you, I'm toast."

"She's toast." Gillian pressed her lips tightly together.

"The thing is . . . I think we should try to gather some evidence—I mean, before you do something crazy like confronting her. I know firsthand how slippery Riley can be. She can turn things against you"—she snapped her fingers—"just like that."

"What kind of evidence?"

"Maybe we should confront Brandon."

Gillian nodded. "Yeah, that's not a bad idea."

"It would sure help if you knew the results of your blood test that night."

"Okay, I'll call my lawyer tomorrow." She looked curiously at Lishia. "If it turns out I was slipped something . . . would you come with me to confront Brandon?"

Lishia took in a quick breath. "I, uh, I guess so. But to be honest, I'm not a great one at confrontations."

Gillian let out a small laugh. "You could've fooled me the night of Todd's birthday. You were pretty confrontational."

Lishia felt bad now. "That was an act . . . one that I'm sorry about."

"Well, maybe you can pull it off again."

They talked for about an hour, putting together a plan for confronting Brandon, and by the time Gillian took Lishia home, Lishia felt like they were almost friends. Almost. But once Gillian found out how much deeper Lishia was into this thing, any hopes of friendship would evaporate.

❧

Lishia tossed and turned all night long, and even when she did manage to fall asleep, she was awakened by a nightmare—a nightmare where she'd been naked and cold and running for her life with bleeding feet. Finally, at around seven in the morning, she gave up on the possibility of sleeping. Maybe this was part of the price one paid for living a big fat lie.

Pacing back and forth in her room, she wondered about her fate. She knew that her life was about to start unraveling. Maybe it had already begun when she'd made her partial confession to Gillian last night. Lishia knew she needed help—serious help. She went over to the Bible on her nightstand, where it had sat untouched for weeks. She traced the lines of a cross through the film of dust on the cover, then decided to open it. The Bible opened to the Gospel of Matthew, and her eyes fell to a verse she had highlighted in pink—probably last summer.

> Don't store up treasures on earth! Moths and rust can destroy them, and thieves can break in and steal them. Instead, store up your treasures in heaven, where moths and rust cannot destroy them, and thieves cannot break in and steal them. Your heart will always be where your treasure is. (Matt. 6:19–21)

She read the words several times, trying to let them sink in. She had previously thought these verses were about money and how she shouldn't put her trust in material things. But suddenly she understood the words differently. As if a lightbulb had gone on inside her head, she knew that Jesus was talking about how she needed to treasure the things of God—to place them over everything else. And she knew she had stopped doing that. Feeling hungry for more, she read on through the next several verses.

> Your eyes are like a window for your body. When they are good, you have all the light you need. But when your eyes are bad, everything is dark. If the light inside you is dark, you surely are in the dark. You cannot be the slave of two masters! You will like one more than the other or be more loyal to one than the other. (Matt. 6:22–24)

That was exactly how she felt! Like her eyes had been full of darkness and everything inside of her was black and moldy and sick and nasty. She set her Bible on her bed and actually got down on her knees, like she used to do as a little girl. Then she bowed her head and confessed what she'd been doing. "I am truly, truly sorry," she said with tears streaming down her cheeks. "Please forgive me. I don't want to serve two masters anymore. I know I was serving Riley, trying to make her happy, but all it brought me was trouble—and heartache and messes. From now on, I only want to serve you, God."

She prayed for a while, pouring out all the sadness and frustrations and fears that had been eating at her the past few weeks. Finally she had no more words, so she said amen and stood, and although her knees felt sore, her spirit felt lighter than ever. She knew that no matter what kind of fallout was coming her way, she could handle it. With God by her side, she would get through it. But the next thing she had to do—and it wouldn't be easy—was to confess to her parents.

She found them having coffee in the breakfast nook. Dad had the newspaper spread in front of him, and Mom was reading Christmas cards. "Do you guys have a minute?" she asked in a voice that sounded small and frightened—almost as if she were a six-year-old.

They both looked up with curious expressions that quickly changed to concerned. "What's wrong?" Mom asked gently.

"I have something to tell you," Lishia began, "and it's not going to be easy."

Dad set the paper aside. "Go ahead."

She began to pour out the whole horrible story, confessing how Riley had connived to get Lishia onto the squad and how Lishia hadn't realized it from the beginning, but when she did know, she still went along with it. She told about how most of the cheerleaders broke the conduct code and even about how she tried a drink last week and how badly it turned out. She knew her parents were shocked to hear all this, but she continued talking, pouring it all out until there was nothing left to say.

"Wow . . ." Dad let out a long sigh.

"Yeah . . ." Mom nodded. "Ditto."

"I know you're both disappointed in me," Lishia said.

"I can't believe you'd do something like that," Mom said sadly. "It doesn't seem like you."

Lishia shrugged. "I guess everyone has the potential to turn into a jerk."

"My question is . . . " Dad removed his glasses, rubbing the bridge of his nose. "What do you plan to do about this?"

"I'll tell Mrs. Glassman the truth . . . and take the consequences."

"When?" Mom asked.

Lishia slumped down into a chair and shook her head. "I don't know."

"School isn't back in session until January," Mom said.

"I know."

"I have another question," Dad said. "What about this boy, the one you think may have slipped a mickey into your drink? What about the consequences for him?"

"Good question," Mom said.

Lishia explained about how she and Gillian would confront him together. "That is, if Gillian's drug test shows that she was given something."

"I find it hard to believe Gillian is even speaking to you." Mom looked doubtful. "Considering everything."

Lishia confessed that Gillian didn't know the whole story yet.

"Yet?" Dad frowned.

"I'll tell her . . . eventually." Lishia closed her eyes and groaned. "I don't have it all figured out yet." A lump was growing in her throat as she felt Mom's hand on her shoulder.

"Well, it's a lot to figure out," Mom said in a choked voice.

Lishia opened her eyes and looked at Mom. She couldn't believe that Mom had tears in her eyes. "I'm sorry I hurt you like this. And I feel rotten that I dumped it all on you a few days before Christmas too. I'm so sorry."

Mom nodded. "It's a lot to take in, Lish. And I have to admit I'm experiencing a lot of different emotions right now."

"Me too," Dad added.

"I feel angry and hurt," Mom confessed. "And disappointed and embarrassed." She shook her head. "And then there's your grandmother and the family . . . and I sent out that Christmas letter, bragging to everyone about how you were a cheerleader now. Oh, Lishia, I can't believe you did this to us."

"I'm sorry, Mom." Now Lishia was crying again.

"Look," Dad said firmly, "the important thing is that you're telling the truth now, Lishia. Somehow we'll all get through this."

They talked about it some more. Naturally, her parents had more questions, more concerns . . . and finally, after it seemed they were all equally frustrated, Dad suggested they pray about it together. Lishia felt relieved when they all bowed their heads and Dad said a brief but sincere prayer.

"We'll survive this, Lishia," he assured her when they were done. "It's not fun and it's not pretty, but we will all learn and grow from it in the end."

Lishia thanked them. "I'm lucky to have such great parents," she said.

"Blessed," Mom corrected. "Luck had nothing to do with it."

She smiled at them both. "Okay, blessed then. I am blessed."

She knew that was true. And she knew she'd taken some good steps today. But she knew the hardest part was still ahead of her. The only thing that would get her through it would be to hold tightly to God's hand. This time she was not going to let go!

eighteen

That night, Lishia went to youth group. It was the first time she'd been in weeks, and the reception she received was different, perhaps even a little chilly in places. She sensed that some of her friends (like Janelle, Chelsea, and Megan) were questioning her presence there, maybe even judging her because they knew what she'd gotten herself into last weekend—and as far as they knew, she was still living a big fat lie. Other old friends were treating her as if she were really special, as if her new status as a cheerleader had elevated her in their eyes. In a way, that seemed even worse than the way Janelle, Chelsea, and Megan were acting. But she didn't hold it against them. After all, not long ago, she'd been just as shallow.

She waited nervously until the time for personal sharing came—then she took in a deep breath and raised her hand up high.

"Hey, Lishia," Raymond said in a warm tone. "Great to have you back again. And congrats on being a cheerleader now. I was at the game last night, and you looked great—too bad the basketball team's not doing better. Anyway, we're all proud of you. Now what did you want to say?"

She cleared her throat and stood. "I just wanted to make a confession." She could hear the nervous tremor in her voice. "Believe me, it's not an easy one to make. But I know that since you are my brothers and sisters in Christ, you will understand . . . and you will forgive me. Anyway, I want to confess to everyone that I have been a great big fraud—a complete phony—and I haven't liked myself at all." The room got so silent she could hear the clock on the back wall ticking.

"I want to admit that I got on the cheerleading squad through false means and say that I plan to confess this to everyone as soon as I can. I expect to be suspended from the squad and maybe even from school . . . and, well, it's all going to be very humiliating." She paused to steady herself, seeing the stunned expressions on the faces, some of which seemed truly empathetic.

"But I don't care that I'm going to look like a fool," she continued, "because today I decided it was time to get honest with myself and with God. I've confessed my sins and repented. And now I want to be honest with everyone else as well—even though it's not easy." She sat down, and leaning forward with her eyes on her lap, she tried not to cry.

"Well, that is very interesting," Raymond said from up front, "because it just so happens to go right along with tonight's message—which is about being transparent with God *and* your friends. So I really appreciate you sharing like you did just now, Lishia. And you can be sure that I—and hopefully everyone else—will really be praying for you in the coming week. Now is there anyone else who would like to share?"

To Lishia's surprise, one after another began to stand up and spill out some pretty hard stories. It was like she'd opened the door, and now everyone started to confess various parts of their lives where they felt like they'd been phonies and frauds and hypocrites. It was all rather eye-opening and amazing.

"I hope everyone will respect and appreciate that there is an unspoken understanding that we are like a family and this is a place of trust. We've had plenty of talks about gossiping, and I sure don't want to hear about anyone here violating that trust." Heads nodded, and Raymond began his message, which he said he would keep short since he felt their personal testimonies were even more valuable than his sermon.

"Now I want us to break up into small groups," he told them after he finished, "and I want us to really pray for each other. I have a feeling this is God's way of giving each and every one of us a special Christmas present this year. What could be better than a clean slate and a fresh spiritual beginning? I hope you'll all participate and receive this gift!"

Lishia ended up in a group with Megan and Chelsea and Grayson. They all shared a little more, and she was touched by their sincerity as they prayed for each other. It really seemed that they sincerely cared about each other. She was also relieved to remember that no one would be in school next week, so the chances of rumors spreading (like to Riley) before she could come clean with Mrs. Glassman and Gillian seemed fairly remote. Even so, she was prepared for the worst just in case that happened.

On Monday morning, Lishia and Mom worked together to track down Mrs. Glassman's home phone number, and Lishia called, asking for the chance to speak to her in person. "I'm sorry to disturb you during Christmas break," she said, "but what I have to say is pretty urgent." When Mrs. Glassman balked at Lishia's invitation to meet for coffee, Mom stepped in.

"I'm sorry too," Mom told her. "I'm a teacher like you, and I wouldn't enjoy hearing from one of my students, but Lishia is telling the truth when she says it's rather urgent."

Fortunately, this seemed to carry some weight, and about an hour later the three of them met at Starbucks and Lishia unloaded the whole sordid tale—and Mrs. Glassman took furious notes. Lishia's plan had been to tell her story without using specific names or implicating anyone else. It was her confession to make, and she didn't want to come across as a tattletale.

"I know this will mean I'm suspended," she said finally. "And I understand that. Mostly I'm really, really sorry for the trouble this will cause you as well as the squad."

Mrs. Glassman looked partly stunned and partly irritated. "I'm sorry too, Lishia. But this opens up a whole new can of worms. Now, like it or not, you are going to have to tell me who else was involved in this scam. I need to know who tampered with the votes. Otherwise, I will be forced to take the whole thing to the administration for even further disciplinary actions—and eventually the name or names will come out. Do you understand me?"

Lishia looked at Mom.

"I think she's right," Mom told her. "You've put Mrs. Glassman in an awkward position. It seems like it's your responsibility to be forthcoming with all the information."

"But I didn't want to rat anyone out," Lishia explained.

"My husband is an attorney," Mrs. Glassman told them. "If this were a legal matter, I think you would be considered an accomplice, at the very least, and if you were put on the witness stand, you would be required to tell the whole truth, Lishia. Or else face perjury charges."

"Just tell her," Mom urged. "You might as well."

Lishia reluctantly told the complete story, including how Gillian's drink, as well as her own, might have been spiked with an illegal drug.

Mrs. Glassman groaned. "The plot thickens."

Lishia nodded.

"So, tell me, were all the cheerleaders participating in these drinking parties?"

"No," Lishia said quickly. Then she listed the girls, including Amanda, who never went to those kinds of parties. "At least as far as I know. This is all pretty new to me."

Mrs. Glassman made note of this.

"Riley doesn't know that I'm confessing," Lishia said quietly.

Mrs. Glassman looked suspicious. "Yes, I thought you and Riley were pretty chummy."

"Riley was forcing Lishia to be her best friend with the threat of blackmail," Mom said defensively.

"Riley said she'd tell you I did the whole thing myself," Lishia said, "when I threatened to go forward and tell you. She said she could make it look like I did it—and that it would seem I had more motive than she did."

"Did you?"

Lishia shrugged. "It might seem that way, but the truth is I've felt trapped for weeks now. I've been miserable. I feel like I sold my soul to the devil."

"Why do you think Riley did this?" Mrs. Glassman peered intently at Lishia.

"Because she can?" Lishia shook her head. "And because she thought she could buy my friendship, and she could control me, and she hated Gillian . . . but mostly I'm starting to think it really was because she could get away with it. Like she was on some kind of power trip. Gillian says she's passive-aggressive, but I don't actually know what that means."

Mrs. Glassman gave a half smile. "So you're speaking to Gillian then?"

Lishia told about their conversation on Friday. "But I didn't tell Gillian everything then. I plan to tell her. And I'm pretty sure she won't be speaking to me when she hears the whole truth."

"Oh, what tangled webs we weave." Mrs. Glassman set down her pen and picked up her coffee. "Is that it, or is there something else I should know?"

"I think that's it." Lishia bit her lip. "But I really am sorry."

"Yes . . ." Mrs. Glassman reached for her bag. "So am I."

On their way home from Starbucks, Lishia called Gillian's number, trying to think of a way to begin what was going to be another tough conversation as she listened to the ringing tones.

"Hey, Lishia," Gillian said cheerfully. "I was just about to call you."

"Really?"

"Yeah. I just spoke to my lawyer, and she got the results from the drug and alcohol tests back."

"And?"

"I had high levels of GHB in my bloodstream."

"GHB?"

"There's a really long medical name for it—gamma-hydroxy-something-or-other—but its street name is Liquid Ecstasy, and it's known as a date rape drug."

"Seriously?"

"I told my lawyer that you and I planned to confront Brandon, and she would like to be there with us. Is that okay with you?"

"Sure, I guess so. But do you think Brandon will be willing to talk if she's there?"

"She said he might clam up but that she'll give him some free legal advice—like how he may need to get himself a lawyer. Anyway, the upside is that this might help to clear my name. Especially if you confront him too. It would be easy to deny that he'd pulled this once, but twice . . . well, that carries some weight."

"Well, I'm happy to help." Lishia knew that she would still have to come clean by confessing her own actions and that Gillian might want to sic her lawyer on her next. But at least she could help Gillian with Brandon first.

"My lawyer can make time for us at four o'clock. Will that work for you?"

"Sure. How do we get Brandon on board?"

"I thought I'd leave that to you. Since you're still a cheer-leader and supposedly Riley's best friend, you have the inside track. Maybe you could ask him to meet you or come to your house or something. Then my lawyer and I would pop in, and we'd all sit down and talk—nice and cozy."

Lishia giggled nervously. "This sounds kinda bizarre—Brandon and me having some clandestine meeting right out of the blue. What if he suspects something?"

"You have to make it sound innocent—maybe act like you're into him or something. He'd love that. Anyway, just get him there. Okay?"

"I'll do what I can."

After she hung up, she explained the crazy plan to Mom. "I don't know what to do," she confessed. "I don't really want to lie to him."

"Didn't you say that he'd acted like he was romantically interested in you at that Christmas party?"

"Yeah, that's right."

"How about if you take it from there? You wouldn't even have to lie. You could simply say something like, 'Remember how you were interested—'"

"Yeah! I could say that I had a hard time remembering what happened that night, which is true, but that I thought he was into me and maybe we should talk about it."

"But where do you plan to meet with him?" Mom asked as she pulled into the driveway.

"Right here," Lishia declared. "I'll think of a reason to ask him to come over."

"And I'll be here too," Mom said, "to listen in the wings."

It was surprisingly easy to get Brandon to agree to meet with her. She used the line her mom suggested, and when he took the bait, she casually said she'd been wanting to do some Christmas shopping, which was true. Brandon offered to take her anytime she liked, and she suggested he stop by her house around four. "Sounds great, can't wait," he said cheerfully.

The plan was that she and Brandon would have a soda in the kitchen. Meanwhile, Mom would phone Gillian so that she and the lawyer could drop in on them. But by the time

Brandon arrived, Lishia was so nervous that she wished she'd put on an extra coating of antiperspirant.

"Mind if we get a soda first?" she said. "I'm parched."

"Sounds good." He followed her into the kitchen. "It's so cool you called, Lishia. I was thinking about you a lot last week, but I was worried you might be mad at me."

"Why would I be mad at you?" she asked, then instantly wished she hadn't since Gillian and the attorney weren't here yet.

"Just the way you were acting, like I'd done something to offend you." He gave her an innocent smile.

"Oh, I was in a snit last week. I think I was just mad at everyone."

He laughed. "Yeah, that's kind of what Riley told me."

She opened the fridge, distracting him by choosing sodas and making small talk about how soon Christmas would be here and how she hadn't had a chance to get her parents any gifts yet. "Cheerleading has taken up so much of my time," she chattered on. "I can't believe how much work it's been to catch up with the rest of the squad. And then there are regionals right after New Year's, and there's going to be all kinds of practice before—"

"Lishia," Mom called. "A friend's here to see you."

"I'm in the kitchen," Lishia called back.

"Maybe that's Riley." Brandon smiled like this would be a good thing.

"Gillian," Lishia tried to act natural.

"What are you doing here?" Brandon frowned.

"We stopped by to talk," Gillian coolly told him.

"I'm Sandra Anthony." The woman behind Gillian handed a business card to Brandon. "Gillian's attorney."

"Huh?" Brandon gave Lishia a worried glance.

"We just want to chat with you." Lishia gestured toward the breakfast nook. "Let's all sit down."

Almost as if they were rounding him up, the three females escorted a surprised-looking Brandon over to the table, cornering him on the closed-in banquette seat with Lishia beside him and Gillian across.

Sandra immediately began with Gillian's blood test results, explaining what GHB was and speculating on how Gillian had it in her system. "Which brings us to Lishia." She nodded to Lishia now, indicating it was her turn to speak.

"Yes, as you know, Brandon, a very similar incident happened with me. You were the one who got me my drink at Vanessa's parents' house. And I suspect if we asked around, there are others who know that you got my drink, and—"

"What are you trying to do?" Brandon looked trapped now. "Should I be calling a lawyer?"

"I would advise you to seek legal counsel," Sandra soberly told him. "Unless you want to cooperate with us and completely disclose your story in an affidavit. In that case, Gillian might reconsider pressing charges." She glanced at Lishia now. "I can't speak for your other alleged victim. However, giving girls what is commonly known as a date rape drug is a serious offense, Mr. Procter, and I doubt that the DA will take these accusations lightly."

Brandon's freckled face was reddening, and Lishia wondered if he was about to start crying. "It was Riley's idea," he told them. "She gave me the stuff. She never told me it was a date rape drug. She just said it would loosen the person up. She wanted Gillian to loosen up so she'd end up doing something stupid. But all I did was put some in her drink. I never planned to rape her." He looked at Gillian with scared eyes. "Honest."

Gillian scowled. "What you did got me into a lot of trouble, Brandon."

"I'm sorry."

"And what about Lishia?" Gillian pressed him.

"It was Riley's idea too."

"Riley was behind that too?" Lishia was shocked. "Why?"

"She said she wanted you to loosen up and have a good time at the party. We didn't know you were going to go nuts on us."

"That stuff made me sick," Lishia told him. "So sick my friends almost took me to the hospital."

"Do you realize how serious this is?" Sandra asked him. "If these girls press charges, you will be in—"

"I'm really, really sorry." Now Brandon actually did start crying. "But, honestly, it was Riley's idea. She made it seem like a big joke—" A choked sob escaped. "Like no big deal. You guys were supposed to be her friends, right? Friends do crazy stuff like that. For laughs, you know." He wiped his nose on his sleeve. "I'm sorry. Really, I am."

"Are you willing to come with me to make a statement?" Sandra asked.

"Will it get me into more trouble?"

"It might keep you from getting into as much trouble," she said gently. "If you like, you can call your parents or a lawyer."

"Do I need a lawyer?"

She stood. "You might."

It wasn't long until they were all gone. Lishia couldn't believe it had been that easy to get Brandon to confess. But maybe he, like her, was sick of the lies and the games . . . maybe he was tired of being one of Riley's pawns. Thinking of Riley only reminded her that she had been ignoring her calls and texts. The last person she wanted to talk to was Riley. Yet she knew it was inevitable.

nineteen

Lishia knew that before she talked to Riley, she needed to come clean with Gillian. It seemed only fair—plus it gave her a good excuse to ignore Riley's numerous text messages, which were growing increasingly obnoxious. However, her palms got sweaty as she punched in Gillian's cell phone number on Monday evening. And then, before she could explain anything, Gillian began gushing about how awesome it was that Lishia had helped to get Brandon to confess.

"He made a complete statement to Sandra once we got to her office," she said happily. "I can't believe how great you were today, Lishia. Seriously, you are the best friend ever! This is really going to help my case."

"I'm glad," Lishia said in a quiet voice.

"You don't sound glad. Are you okay?"

"I, uh, I have something I need to tell you, Gillian. But I wonder if I should tell you in person." Lishia didn't really want to have a face-to-face conversation, but she'd heard somewhere, maybe in church, that that was the right way to clear things up with a person you'd offended.

"What is it?"

"Do you really want me to tell you over the phone?" Although it was appealing, she knew it was the coward's way out.

"Well, you've got me dying of curiosity now, Lishia. So, yeah, just tell me."

"I wanted to tell you this on Friday, but I was hoping to, uh, deal with some other things first." Lishia bumbled along for a bit, stumbling over her words until she realized she was sounding more and more idiotic.

"What are you trying to say?" Gillian finally demanded.

Lishia poured out the whole ugly story, cringing all over again to hear what a stupid fool she'd been to trust someone like Riley and at the same time wishing for the day when she could put all this behind her. How many more times would she have to repeat this embarrassing tale?

"You've got to be kidding!" Gillian's voice was a mix of disbelief and anger.

"I wish I was kidding, Gillian. But I really am sorry. Really, really sorry."

"Sorry . . . yeah . . . right." Gillian's voice had a flat sound to it now. Lishia could tell she was hurt—she probably felt like Lishia had pulled the rug out from under her.

"Honestly, Gillian, I'd do anything to turn back the clock and make it so all this never happened. I know you so much better now and I never—" She heard a loud click, the sound of a phone being snapped shut. "Gillian?" she said meekly. No answer. Of course, Gillian had hung up on her. And why shouldn't she?

Lishia closed her own phone, then sat down on her bed and wondered what, if anything, she could do to soften this thing with Gillian. Was there anything more she could do to take some of the sting away? She really liked Gillian now—and knowing that she'd hurt her so badly made Lishia feel sick inside. When would this mess end?

Lishia went to her closet and looked at the cheerleader clothing hanging neatly together. Of course—she would return all of Gillian's stuff! Never mind that Mom and Lishia had paid for it; it was obvious that Lishia wouldn't need it anymore. In fact, it would be a relief to be rid of it. So she got some bags and neatly folded everything to fill three bags. While it was mostly a relief, she also felt some sadness as she realized that her chances of being part of the squad were truly gone. Not only had she blown it . . . it had never been meant to be.

Next she sat down and wrote Gillian an apology letter. She took her time and went into more detail, explaining how she'd been pulled into the whole scheme, how she had wanted to stop it when she realized that Riley had tampered with the votes, and how she'd eventually succumbed to what was essentially blackmail. But finally she admitted that she really couldn't blame Riley for everything since Lishia had made her own choices. Still, she said one last time, she was sorry. Very, very sorry. She put the three-page letter in an envelope and tucked it inside one of the bags. Gillian would probably just tear it up—like she'd probably tear into Lishia if she ever got the opportunity.

Finally, Lishia explained to Mom what she'd done and asked her to drive her to Gillian's house. With a pounding heart, Lishia rang Gillian's doorbell, and when Gillian's mother answered, Lishia quickly apologized to her and handed over the bags. Mrs. Rodowski looked slightly bewildered, but Lishia didn't have the words to explain any further, so she simply turned and hurried back to the car. Neither she nor Mom said a single word on the trip back home. It seemed that all the words had already been said. And really, Lishia was sick of words.

⌘

To Lishia's relief, Riley left town with her family the next day. According to Riley's latest message, which sounded slightly friendlier than the previous ones, the Atkins family would be staying at a fancy ski resort in Montana. "My dad surprised us with this," Riley explained. "We'll be there until New Year's Day. If you and I had been getting along better, I might've asked you to come along. Anyway, Dad says that cell phone service is pretty sketchy there, so I probably won't talk to you until we get home."

Relief rushed through Lishia. She was so thankful for this little reprieve. She sent a simple text message wishing Riley a good Christmas and promising to talk more when Riley got back. But mostly she was glad that Riley was gone. Lishia wasn't ready to sort this out with her yet. She felt emotionally spent now, in need of some peace and quiet.

For the next few days, Lishia was perfectly content to hang at home. She was happy to spend time with her family and help Mom in preparation for Christmas. Oh, she wasn't looking forward to explaining her recent dilemma to her relatives on Christmas Day. But she was ready to get it behind her. At least she would have the support of her parents. That was worth a lot.

Lishia had also been surprised by how supportive Megan had been these past few days. She called to check on Lishia two to three times a day. She even invited her to go ice-skating with some friends on the day before Christmas. At first Lishia said no, she needed to stay home and help with wrapping gifts, but Mom put her foot down, insisting Lishia should go. Once she was there, Lishia couldn't believe how much fun it was to do such an ordinary activity or how great it was being with her old friends. It was almost like they were kids again—and that felt good. Plus it gave Lishia hope. Maybe there really was life after Riley.

On Christmas Day, shortly before they were to sit down at Grandma Willis's big dining table, Lishia stood in front of her extended family and made her embarrassing confession. She'd hoped it might be easier by now, but it was even harder than when she'd done it at youth group. These people had known and supported her for her whole life. They'd believed in her, hoped the best for her, even contributed to her purchasing the uniform.

After she finished, everyone remained really quiet, and it was obvious that some of them were totally shocked, but then Uncle Roy grinned and slapped his thigh and said, "Well, good golly, Lishia, at least you're not pregnant!" He winked at Dad. "That's what I thought she was about to say." Of course, everyone laughed and lightened up. And Lishia felt a tiny bit better.

However, as they ate dinner, she still sensed that some of her relatives were deeply disappointed in her—though probably not as much as she had been disappointed in herself. But fortunately, by the end of the day, when they were all sitting around playing board games and just being goofy, she could tell that they still loved her, and once again she felt extremely thankful for family.

❧

Despite Riley's concerns about "lack of service" at the resort, Lishia had received a couple of chirpy text messages from her. Apparently if they went to a nearby town, her phone would work. Anyway, it sounded like she was having a fantastic time, getting really good at snowboarding, and completely oblivious to Lishia's recent confession to Mrs. Glassman. That was a relief.

Lishia considered giving Riley a little heads up about the whole thing but decided against it. Why ruin Riley's family vacation? Riley's life would fall apart soon enough. At least that's what Lishia assumed. There was always the off chance that Mrs. Glassman would choose to handle this in a different way. Lishia had no idea how she would react if that happened. How would she feel if Riley came out of this mess unscathed? Sometimes Lishia had suspected that Riley had some kind of Teflon coating, slipping through the stickiest situations while others tripped up and fell on their faces. What if Riley slipped through this one too?

Finally Lishia realized that instead of obsessing over the possibility that Riley's life would continue as usual, she should just keep praying. And because she didn't know exactly how to pray—for Riley—she turned her prayer into a short one. Whenever she thought of Riley, she simply prayed, *God's will be done in Riley's life.* It was the only prayer she could manage that didn't make her feel like throwing something. And it was genuine. She did want God's will for Riley.

A couple days after Christmas, Lishia went to the next

scheduled cheerleading practice. Not to practice, since that was ridiculous, but to apologize to the other girls and explain why she was off the squad. Practice was supposed to be in the gym, which was opened due to the guys' basketball practice. However, Lishia was surprised to see that Mrs. Glassman was not present. Even more surprising was that the other girls were completely in the dark as to what had happened with Lishia. She'd barely begun her apology when they started questioning her.

"What do you mean you're not practicing today?" Vanessa demanded to know. "We have work to do!"

"I already told you, I'm off the squad," Lishia repeated. "I came by to say I'm sorry and explain that—"

"But we need you," Amanda insisted. "You know we're getting ready for regionals right now. It's bad enough that Riley's gone for all of Christmas break. But how can we practice without you too?"

"You'll have to figure it out," Lishia told her. "And really, I'm sorry. I never meant for—"

"So what exactly happened?" Krista asked. "Why are you off?"

Lishia had been determined not to tell the entire story (it didn't seem right to tell the part about Riley's involvement) but to simply take the blame for her own mistakes. "I was trying to explain. I've been suspended—"

"Why?" Amanda asked.

"Is it because of what happened at my parents' party?" Vanessa's eyes got wide, like she was worried now. "Because it's not like I told Glassman anything. No one did."

"To be honest, it's partly because of that," Lishia admitted.

"But that's not fair." Amanda glanced at Vanessa. "There

were other girls at your party too—including you. And no one else was suspended."

"How long are you suspended for?" Krista asked.

"I'm off," Lishia said slowly. "For good."

"But what about—"

"I'm really sorry," Lishia said again. She had wanted to do this without tears, but they were threatening to come. Still, she didn't want to break down in front of everyone. "Honestly, if there was any way to keep this from happening, I would. But it's over, okay? I just wanted to tell you guys in person—and to say that I'm truly sorry and I hope everything turns out okay." She tried to step away, but they continued to press around her.

Everyone continued talking at once. Some of the girls sounded confused, worried over their own cheerleader status. Others, like Amanda and Krista, sounded outraged, and justly so. But Lishia could tell there was no use trying to explain anymore. Besides, the tears had escaped and she felt even more embarrassed. She hadn't expected this to be so hard, but it wasn't easy letting others down.

"I'm sorry," she said one last time. Then she turned and ran out of the gym, out the door, and to the street where Mom's car was still waiting.

"Was that pretty hard?" Mom asked.

Lishia nodded as she sniffed noisily.

"Well, at least it's behind you."

"Uh-huh."

Mom handed her a tissue from her purse. "Remember, you're moving forward now, Lishia. It will get better."

"Yeah, but I still have Riley to deal with. Chances are she'll hear about this now that the others know. Her cell phone doesn't work at the ski resort, but she gets to a place where she can send and receive messages." She blew her nose. "She'll hear about this soon enough."

"And when she does, you will deal with it."

"Yeah . . . I guess so."

Despite how hard it had been to tell the cheerleaders, Lishia felt a sense of relief to know that it was over. And for a change, she could actually sleep through the night without waking up with a panic attack. As a result, she spent the next few days catching up on sleep—as well as praying and reading her Bible. She felt like she was having her own spiritual awakening, and it felt good. She also spent some time with Megan, who was turning into a very loyal friend—not to mention an excellent listener. And by New Year's Eve day, Lishia felt stronger than she'd felt in months. Not only was there a light at the end of her tunnel, but she felt as if she'd actually passed through the darkness and was starting to bask in that clean, warm light. And it felt good!

However, she felt somewhat caught off guard, even blindsided, when she answered the doorbell to see Gillian standing on her front porch with a hard-to-read expression on her face. "Oh?" Lishia blinked in surprise. "Uh . . . what are you doing here?"

"I came to talk to you. Can I come in?"

"Sure." Lishia opened the door wider.

"Don't worry, it's not like I came over here to knock your lights out." Gillian made a sarcastic-sounding laugh. "Although that did go through my mind last week."

"I don't really blame you," Lishia nervously admitted as she led Gillian into the family room. "Uh, do you want a soda or anything?"

"No." Gillian flopped down on a chair, then stared at Lishia without saying a thing.

"So . . . ?" Lishia sat down on the edge of the couch and waited nervously.

"So . . . as you probably know, I was infuriated at you after that phone call. I mean seriously angry. And don't get me wrong, I was furious with Riley too. In fact, I was so outraged that I wanted to get totally wasted."

Lishia took in a quick breath. "Oh no!"

"But I didn't."

Lishia slowly exhaled. "I'm so glad."

"Me too." Gillian gave a half smile. "Yeah, I realized that would be like trying to hurt you and Riley by beating myself in the head with a sledgehammer. Not terribly smart."

Lishia nodded.

"So I talked to my rehab counselor, and she said I needed to forgive you guys." Gillian shook her head. "But that's a lot easier said than done."

"I can imagine. The truth is, I'm still mad at Riley, and I'm trying to forgive her too."

"Anyway, I told my counselor it would be easier to forgive you than Riley. At least you apologized to me." She pressed her lips together. "And thanks for returning my old uniforms . . . not that I can use them. But it's kinda nice to get them back."

"It seemed like the least I could do."

"So anyway, I got up this morning and decided that I would try to forgive you—you know, bury the hatchet before the New Year begins."

"Really?" Lishia brightened.

"Yeah. I guess I kind of understand what happened . . . I

get how Riley could've pulled you into her nasty little web of lies."

"But it was my choice," Lishia admitted. "I need to own that."

"Yeah, that's true."

"But I really appreciate you coming by to tell me that, Gillian. You have no idea how much it means to me. I felt so bad when you hung up on me. I mean, I know why you did. I just wish I could undo it. Anyway, thanks for forgiving me."

"It's going to take a lot longer to forgive Riley." She frowned. "If that's even possible."

"I know."

Gillian relaxed a little and began filling Lishia in on how things were going with her lawyer. "Brandon is totally cooperating, and he's actually really sorry. It looks like his affidavit is going to help my case."

As they talked about the situation with Riley, they were surprised at how similar their feelings were. It was more like good therapy than it was gossiping. Finally, Lishia told Gillian she thought there was one good thing that had come out of the whole nasty mess. "For me, anyway."

"What's that?" Gillian asked curiously.

"It made me return to God." Now Lishia explained how she'd turned her back on God last fall. "It was like I traded God for what I thought was going to be the best 'best friend.' Instead, it turned out that Riley was the worst friend I've ever had in my life. Now I realize that God is my very best friend."

Gillian's brow creased. "How is that even possible?"

"Because I go to God with all my problems now." Lishia explained how she could take anything, big or small, to God. How she could pray about things, and how he could lead her if she was listening. "It's so much better than it ever was before. So in a weird way, I'm thankful for all the crud I went through. But at the same time I'm sorry for the way I hurt so many people . . . like you."

Gillian scowled. "Riley's the one who should be sorry."

Lishia nodded. "Yeah . . . but we don't have any control over what Riley does or how she reacts to all this."

"Yeah, I guess I need to remember that." She gave a sheepish smile. "Wanting to have control is one of my issues. It's like I get frustrated over having no control over anything, and that's when I want to drink—you know, to forget everything."

"So what are you doing for New Year's Eve?" Lishia got an idea.

"Well, for sure, I'm not going out drinking." Gillian laughed.

"Want to come to a party at my church?"

Gillian looked disappointed. "A *church* party?"

"It's actually our youth group. There are a few kids you know from school there." She began to list some names. Then she explained that it was mostly a bunch of teens eating junk food, listening to music, playing games, and just having a good time. "And then right before midnight, we'll take a few minutes to sing some songs and pray. So it's not like it's real churchy. You know? Just kids having ordinary fun with no alcohol, no cattiness, and no backstabbing."

Gillian brightened. "I can't believe I'm saying this, but that actually sounds kinda appealing. I think I'd like to go."

"Great. Megan and I will pick you up around eight, okay?"

"Sounds good."

Of course, Megan sounded totally shocked when Lishia told her the good news. "You're kidding! Did I hear you right? Gillian Rodowski is coming to youth group with us tonight?"

"That's right."

"Wow, Lishia, that is very cool."

And it did turn out to be very cool. Everyone was warm and welcoming to Gillian, and she seemed to have a genuinely good time. Even when it was time to sing and pray at midnight, she actually joined in, and after it was all over and done, she thanked Lishia for inviting her. She even promised to come to youth group again. All in all, it seemed a good way to start out a new year.

twenty

Lishia couldn't believe that she didn't hear from Riley the day before school started. She knew Riley's family was supposed to get home the day after New Year's Day, and she fully expected Riley to call the next day—probably in a furious rage. But Lishia's phone never rang. And there were no text messages either. Finally, at around eight that night, Lishia actually tried to call Riley. But her call rolled over to voice mail.

"Uh, Riley, this is Lishia. I just wanted to talk to you. I, uh, I think there's some things you should know about before you go to school tomorrow. Anyway, why don't you give me a call?"

However, Riley never called. But before Lishia went to bed, she said a prayer for her ex–best friend. It was one of those "God's will be done" prayers, but she figured it was better than nothing. Then she went to sleep.

"Are you pretty nervous?" Megan asked as she drove them to school the next day.

"Uh . . . yeah." Lishia bit her lip and tried not to think about what Riley might do when she found out that Mrs. Glassman knew everything.

"Have you heard from Riley yet?"

"No, but I'm actually praying for her today. And more than just God's will be done now. I'm praying that God will use whatever happens as a wake-up call, you know, so she'll realize that he has a better plan for her."

"That's cool that you're praying for her. But I've been praying for you." She gave an uneasy-sounding laugh. "That you survive this day—and Riley."

Lishia tried to laugh, but it came out all wrong. "Thanks . . . I think."

"And really, I'd pray for Riley too." Megan shook her head. "But I'm afraid my prayers wouldn't be very Christlike."

"What would you pray?"

"I'd ask God to give her a good smack down."

Now Lishia did laugh. "To be honest, I feel like that too."

"But what if that doesn't happen? What if she gets away with this? What if she's not kicked off of the squad? What if she makes it look like it's all your fault?"

"Then she gets away with it. I told Mrs. Glassman the truth. There's nothing else I can do about it."

"Fine. Then I'm going to pray that God doesn't let Riley get away with it. I don't care if he gives her a smack down or not, but I hope he won't let her slide. That's not fair. Not to Gillian or to you—and not to any of the other cheerleaders either. Not to mention the real alternates."

Lishia agreed with Megan, but she also knew that sometimes

things happened that weren't fair—sometimes there was nothing you could do about it. That was life. Lishia's legs felt a little shaky as she walked into the school building. She knew she wouldn't be able to avoid Riley today. But how much did Riley know? Was she waiting to pounce on Lishia? Or would Lishia still have to explain everything and then experience the fallout? It was all so stressful, but at least Lishia had used her extra-strong antiperspirant this morning. She would need it.

Glancing around the entryway for Riley, Lishia hurried her way to her locker, hanging up her coat and grabbing a couple of books, hoping to make it to her first class without a confrontation.

"Did you hear there's a meeting?"

Lishia jumped as she saw Riley peering at her with curious eyes. She had a very deep-looking tan on her face, probably the result of the ski vacation. "Oh, hi, Riley. Long time no see." Lishia tried to steady herself, to act normal.

"Yeah, sure, but did you hear about this meeting? It sounds urgent."

Lishia shook her head as she closed her locker. "What meeting?"

"It's with Mrs. Glassman, in her office. Amanda just told me. It's only the varsity cheerleaders—something is definitely up. And we're excused from first period. So come on, let's go see what's going on."

"But I—"

"Come on." Riley eagerly tugged her arm. "Let's hurry so we don't miss anything."

"But I'm not on the squad anymore," Lishia said as she allowed Riley to propel her down the breezeway.

"What?" Riley stopped walking and stared with wide eyes.

"I'm suspended from cheerleading."

"Why?" Riley's eyes narrowed. "What did you do, Lishia?"

Lishia swallowed hard. "I told Mrs. Glassman the truth. I told her that I didn't deserve to be a cheerleader anymore. And now I am officially off and—"

"What the—"

"Look, Riley, it's over and I'm fine with it and I just wanted to tell you—"

"It is *not* over," she seethed. Her grip on Lishia's arm tightened. "Come on, let's get to the bottom of this."

"It's no use, Riley." Lishia decided not to resist, letting Riley pull her toward the athletic department. Maybe this little walk would give her time to explain. "I'm done with cheerleading and I'm glad."

"No, you are not," Riley insisted. "You're delusional."

"Mrs. Glassman knows everything, Riley."

Riley stopped walking again. "What?"

"I didn't want to tell her about your part in it, but she forced me to tell her the whole story. She knows everything, Riley. You need to be prepared for what's going to—"

"What do you mean she knows *everything*?" Riley's eyes got huge. "What are you saying?"

"I mean she knows what you did, Riley. She knows how you tampered with the votes so that I could—"

Riley jerked hard on Lishia's arm now, pulling her right in front of her and glaring into her face. "You better be making this up, Lishia Vance."

"Hey there," a guy's voice said. "Easy does it, Riley."

Lishia looked up to see Grayson joining them. He was followed by Megan and Chelsea and Janelle. Her youth group friends made a semicircle around her and Riley.

"This is between Lishia and me," Riley seethed at him. "Butt out."

"It's over for me, Riley." Lishia tried to move away from her. "Go to the meeting and you'll probably find out that Mrs. Glassman knows everything. I have no idea what she'll do about it, but she does know."

"You ungrateful little bi—" Riley raised her hand with her bag in it, swinging it toward Lishia, but Grayson stopped the bag in midair, and the girls pushed Riley away from Lishia.

"You need to go cool off," Chelsea told Riley.

"Go to your meeting," Megan said. "Find out for yourself what's going on."

"And leave Lishia alone!" Janelle yelled.

Riley looked shocked, and Lishia couldn't help but feel encouraged by the support of her friends. Even Janelle had stuck up for her!

"Fine." Riley straightened herself up, holding her head high. "I'm sure that it's nothing like you're saying, Lishia. I just need to straighten Glassman out. Once she hears my story, she will know that I'm innocent and that you're the one who messed everything up. I should've known not to trust you." She turned and stormed off.

"Wow." Grayson shook his head. "She's a real piece of work."

"You better watch out for that girl," Janelle said with concern.

"Thanks." Lishia smiled weakly at her friends. "I really appreciate your help."

"I'll try to stick closer," Megan promised. "I'll meet you at your locker before lunch. Okay?"

Naturally, Lishia didn't protest.

By the end of the day, the whole school was talking about it. A few had heard twisted versions of the story, but most of them had gotten it somewhat straight. Three cheerleaders had been suspended from the squad. Lishia was off, due to the fact that Riley had tampered with the votes and she never should've been on in the first place. For that reason Riley was no longer a cheerleader either, and she was also suspended from school. It seemed that Mrs. Glassman had found evidence that Riley, while acting as academic assistant, had gotten into her computer more than once.

Lishia was slightly surprised to hear that Vanessa was also suspended from the squad for hosting the drinking party where alcohol was served to minors. Apparently someone else had come forward with this information. And a couple of the other cheerleaders were placed on probation because they had attended that particular party. All in all, it was not a good day for the Kingston Cougars varsity cheerleaders. Lishia felt partly to blame. But only partly.

"You're not going to believe this," Gillian told Lishia when she found her in the locker bay after school.

"What?" Lishia could tell by Gillian's expression that this was good news.

"Mrs. Glassman has asked me to return to cheering!"

"No way!"

"It's true." Gillian nodded with a serious expression. "My attorney sent Mrs. Glassman a letter, explaining about how my case has changed thanks to Brandon's confession. And Mrs. Glassman called me to her office this afternoon. She told me she knows about the other cheerleaders who were partying just like me and how she decided to put them all on probation. They can still cheer, but if they step out of line, they'll be suspended too."

"Yeah, I heard about that," Lishia admitted.

"So she had the squad vote on whether I should be re-instated and placed on probation as well. And they voted to bring me back!" Gillian had tears in her eyes. "Can you believe it?"

Lishia hugged her. "That's awesome, Gillian!"

She nodded. "Unfortunately, they can't reinstate you too."

"I know," Lishia said. And I'm okay with that. After all, I wasn't even a *real* alternate."

"Yeah, that's right. And now Michelle will be on the squad. She's totally jazzed."

"That's great."

"So, anyway, I know I promised to do coffee with you and Megan after school, but I need to go to practice now. We have lots of catching up to do."

"I'm so happy for you, Gillian." Lishia grinned. "Seriously, that's the best news of the day."

"Thanks . . . I mean for everything."

Now Megan came over to join them, and Gillian said she couldn't go for coffee, but Lishia explained why.

"That's so cool," Megan told Gillian. "Congratulations!"

"Thanks." Gillian grinned.

"Make us proud," Lishia said.

"Too bad we don't have a good basketball team to cheer for," Megan teased.

"Doesn't matter." Gillian looped the strap of her duffle bag over a shoulder. "I'm just happy to be cheering again."

As they walked to the car, Megan asked Lishia if she was

worried about Riley coming after her now. "I mean, she must be pretty furious."

"I'm sure she's mad at me, but I'm not too concerned." Lishia shrugged, then smiled. "For starters, I have some pretty good friends helping to watch my back."

"Yeah, that's true."

"But besides that . . ." Lishia sighed. "I know God's looking out for me."

Megan nodded but still looked a little concerned.

"And I think that once Riley realizes it's really over—you know, when it sinks in that she can't control me or manipulate others—well, she'll probably want to keep a low profile for a while. Don't you think?"

"I hope so. And it'll probably help that she's suspended from school for a few days. That'll give her a chance to cool off. But I don't know, Lish, I wouldn't put much of anything past that girl."

"No, me neither. I guess I learned that lesson the hard way." Lishia pulled on her coat. "And as weird as this might sound, I think I learned a lot about friendship from Riley too."

Megan looked doubtful. "How is that possible?"

"I learned that instead of looking for someone to be my best friend, I need to learn how to *become* a best friend myself. Because if I can't *be* a best friend, I probably don't deserve one. You know?"

Megan gave a sheepish smile. "Hey, I'm willing to give you a try . . . I mean as a best friend."

Lishia laughed. "I'd consider that an honor." As they got into the car, Lishia realized that it really would be an honor. Even though she'd never felt like she'd had much in common with Megan in the past, she knew that Megan was truly a good person. And Megan had stood by Lishia during some pretty hard times too. So Lishia decided that she would do this wholeheartedly. She would do everything she could to become a really good best friend to Megan. And with God (aka her very Best Friend) showing her how, she knew it could happen!

MELODY CARLSON is the award-winning author of over two hundred books with sales of more than five million. She is the author of many teen books, including *Just Another Girl*, *Anything but Normal*, *Double Take*, and the Diary of a Teenage Girl series. She is also the author of several Christmas books, including the bestselling *The Christmas Bus*, *The Christmas Dog*, and *Christmas at Harrington's*. Melody was twice nominated for a Romantic Times Career Achievement Award in the inspirational market for her books. She and her husband live in central Oregon. For more information about Melody, visit her website at www.melodycarlson.com.

What if beauty is more than just
skin deep?

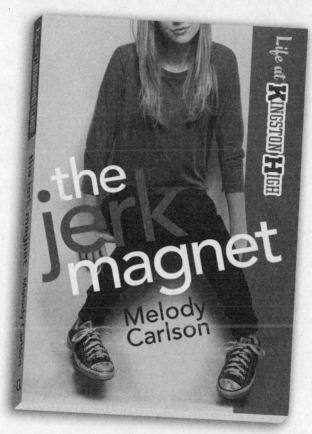

Don't miss the first book in the
Life at Kingston High series!

Revell
a division of Baker Publishing Group
www.RevellBooks.com

Available wherever books are sold.

What do you do when your life's not all it's cracked up to be? Get a new one.

Worlds collide when a Manhattan socialite and a simple Amish girl meet and decide to switch places.

Revell
a division of Baker Publishing Group
www.RevellBooks.com

Available wherever books are sold.

New School = New Chance for That First Kiss

Just when it seems Elise is on top of the world, everything comes crashing down. Could one bad choice derail her future?

Girls know all about keeping secrets,
but Sophie's is a really big one.

anything
but
normal

A NOVEL

Melody Carlson

Visit Melody Carlson at www.melodycarlson.com.

 Revell
a division of Baker Publishing Group
www.RevellBooks.com

Available wherever books are sold.